THE
MALEFICIO
CHRONICLES

CLINT WESTGARD

ALSO BY CLINT WESTGARD

The Shadow Men:

    Realm of Shadows

    Council of Shadows

    Dance of Shadows

The Sojourners Cycle:

    The Forgotten

    The Apostate

    The Acolyte (forthcoming)

    The Double (forthcoming)

    The Sojourner (forthcoming)

The Trials of the Minotaur

The Devious Kind (a mystery)

Published by Lost Quarter Books
www.lostquarterbooks.com

This edition 2016

Cover image from Marriage of Martin de Loyola to Princess Dona
Beatriz and Don Juan Borja to Princess Lorenza, 1718.

ISBN: 978-1-928035-02-2

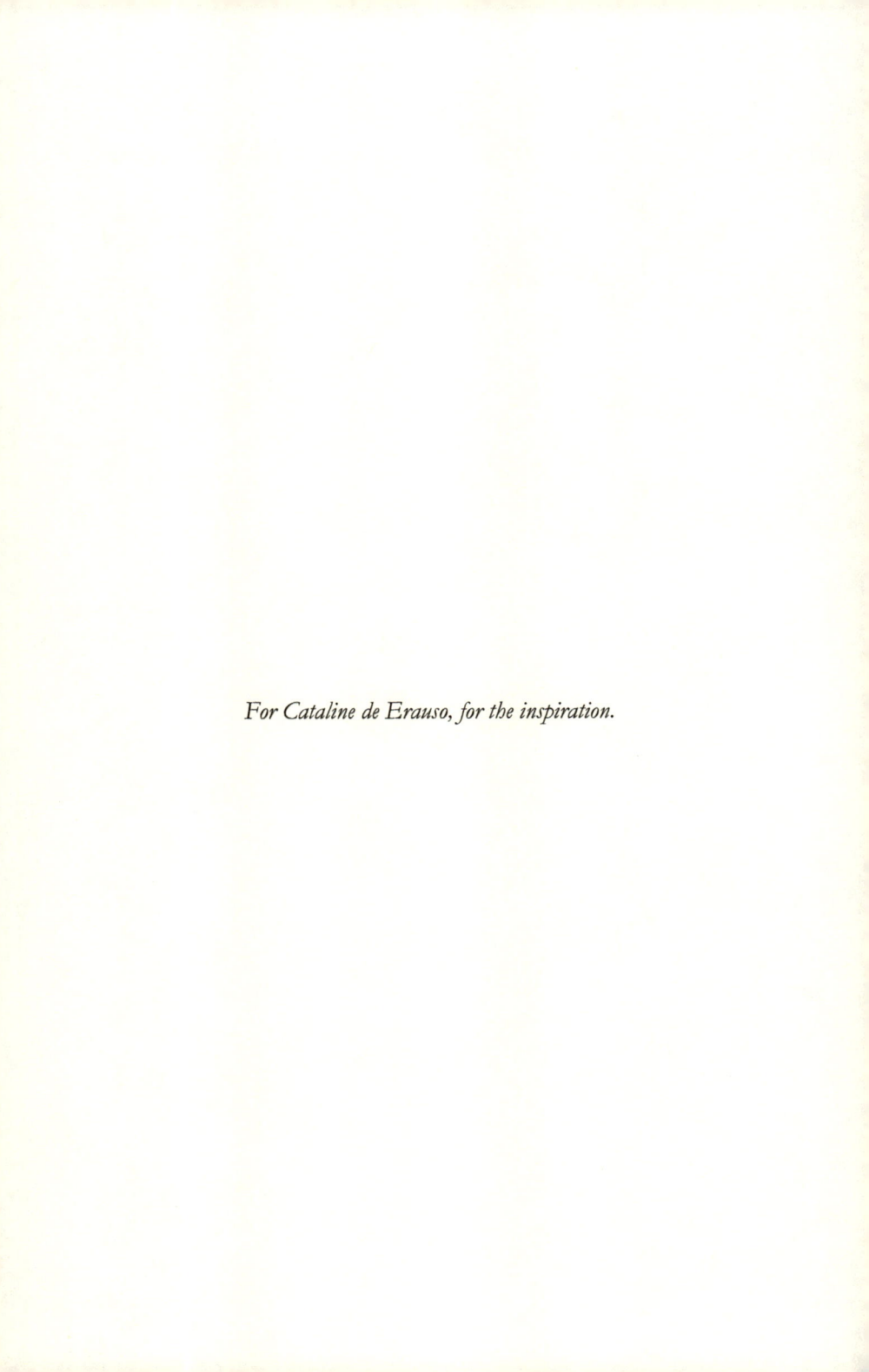

For Cataline de Erauso, for the inspiration.

CONTENTS

AUTHOR'S NOTE

The discovery of the strange record that follows is one of happenstance, as always seems to be the case in such matters. It was some years ago now, back in my days as a graduate student, that I passed a summer researching my dissertation at the Archivo General de la Nación in Lima. The moment was actually one of personal crisis for me, as I had begun to question the very path I had chosen. The completion of my dissertation, some trifling matter on the Inquisition in Peru, had become an insurmountable burden to me, the subject only becoming staler the further I burrowed in. Making matters worse, I knew I had nothing original to say; I would simply be echoing, with a few minor tweaks here and there, the consensus established in all the books I had read on the period.

At the end of that summer I would abandon my studies, not returning to my university that fall and embarking on a journey, the details of which are irrelevant to the matter at hand. To ensure that I had left the land razed and well salted over, I did not inform anyone at my institution of my plans. I simply, as far as they were concerned, disappeared. Readers who follow the story below will perhaps understand where I got my idea from, though at the time I had no sense of the author's influence over me.

I discovered the record mixed in with some of the regular court documents of the Inquisition, accusations of heresy and witchcraft and the like. Those familiar with the institution will no doubt realize this is a singular document. In the brief period of my research I cannot recall coming across anything similar. It is a confession of sorts, though it does not seem to be associated with any case that I could find and has the form of more a personal correspondence. Based on the year the narrator gives for her birth, and some of the other incidental things she mentions, I would place the main events in the record as taking place beginning in 1600 or 1601 in colonial Lima.

A few notes on the historical context follow for those who are unfamiliar with the period in question. The conquest of Peru by Pizarro and his men took place beginning in 1532. Lima, the City of Kings, was founded in 1535. Though the Spanish Crown established the Viceroyalty of Peru in 1542, their control of the territory was tenuous, with the remnants of the Incan empire in a state of revolt for decades. Their authority over even the Spaniards who immigrated to the new colony was nominal, as thousands sought to make their fortunes by any means necessary, while those who had succeeded in that enterprise attempted to transform their humble beginnings into a noble lineage. Into such a family our narrator was born.

MALEFICIO IN THE CLOISTER

I HARDLY KNOW where to begin in a task such as this. I have not written much since my youth in the convent, although then I flattered myself with thinking I was quite skilled at the practice. There was some writing when I was in the employ of Don Tadeo, but it was not of this kind. I have never been interested in stories— beginnings and middles—for one has to arrive at an end from which to gain a vantage point to scan the whole proceedings. I am not the kind to look back or dwell on past moments and their significance. That sort of thing is always changing anyway; the morning has a different hue come evening.

So it is a foreign thing I am doing here, and I beg your forgiveness should the telling go poorly. But you have insisted and I shall comply. I owe you that much anyway. Owe you that and so much more, but these inadequate phrases shall have to suffice. Perhaps you can understand something of this burden that shadows my every step.

I was born into a family of some standing, in the year of Our Lord 1585 in Lima, whose name I will not mention, for their honor will have suffered enough from my various transgressions. We had a large estate in one of the finer neighborhoods of that fair city, surrounded by towering walls that sheltered us from any prying eyes. Those walls delineated the universe of my childhood, for I rarely left the estate, and my only time out of doors was spent in the crafted and manicured gardens of the estate grounds.

My childhood was one of shadow and darkness. The sunlight

3

gave my mother severe headaches and she spent most her days in bed. The windows in her wing of the estate had to be shuttered and covered with blinds in case she should happen to emerge, leaving most of the house off-limits to her. I was her only child and, with no real friends or companions among the rest of the household, I spent most of my days near her quarters in the often vain hope that she would be well enough to invite me into her chambers. There I would listen as she recounted tales of our family's remarkable history.

My father I remember as a distant, pained figure who rarely strayed to my mother's rooms. I cannot recall more than three words that he said to me directly. My very presence seemed to wound him. He had two other daughters, both older than I, whom the servants and my cousins doted on. Me they avoided, whispering to each other when I would pass them in the hall.

One of my clearest memories of that time is of a conversation I managed to overhear in my father's quarters. I cannot call to mind how I came to be there, hidden in the cove beneath his writing desk and behind the desk's chair—no doubt I was in the midst of some childish game, for I was no more than ten—but there I was as two of the house servants stole an embrace and then shared a confidence.

That woman is a seductress. She has used sorcery on the Don. This from the woman, a scullery girl and a mulata, who should not have been in my father's quarters, though the same could have been said of me.

Yes, she has clearly done evil to him with her spells. This was one of my father's servants, an Indian boy.

And that child is of the same kind. Those words have never left me; they come to my thoughts unbidden, in those moments when I am unguarded from drink or despair. That was the first I became aware I was different from others in some fundamental way and that this was the reason for the unkindness, the whispers and the evil glares. How they feared me! Their hatred gave me strength that still carries me through my days, even as my steps have grown heavier with each year.

Mother was never long for this world, so it seemed to me. I have been told she was once one of Lima's most beautiful women, but she had faded from that glory by the time I can remember her. Her skin was always a spectral shade, her breathing labored and her eyes unfocused. In her last year of life she was rarely coherent, subsiding often into a fever-like state where she would rave about those in San Sebastién, who had conspired against her and condemned her to this exile. She told me, in one of her final lucid moments before she succumbed to the pox that swept through Lima that winter, how sorry she was that she would not have more time with me. Though I was young, I understood what her meaning was.

There was so much I was going to teach you, she told me. So much you needed to learn. The world will be difficult for you. It was for me. That is our lot. I only hope you do more than I have with what you have been given.

I do not know if I have succeeded in this regard. My life has been a series of wrong turns, each leading me further astray. Who knows what the future offers, though I fear you will have more to say in that regard than I. Perhaps that is for the best, given all I have done.

I fear my thoughts have overwhelmed me, this pen, so burdensome; it has dragged my spirit down to a step before damnation. What a punishment you have devised for me! You would say it is no such thing, that it is for my and your edification. I have not thought of these times in many years. They were not kind to me, though few times have been, as you shall see. Onward.

Following my mother's death I was sent to pass the remainder of my days in Convent of La Encarnación. I was eleven or twelve perhaps, and my father had long determined that I was not suitable material for marriage. His family name was at stake. I would have been sent to a monastery earlier, I am certain, had my mother not opposed it. I was her only true companion in those last years. With her gone there was nothing left for me in that home and there had been so little happiness, even when she was alive, that I went to the convent gladly. Our family was important enough that my dowry was easily paid for and I was ensconced as a novice in its enclosure.

But I should say something of the convent itself before I continue with my tale, for I know from our discussions that these things hold some interest for you. La Encarnación, as you no doubt know, was one of the oldest monasteries in the City of Kings, and it was situated to the east of the Plaza de Armas and the government buildings, near the Rimac River. As with all convents, it had the look of a fortress to it, with stout and resolute walls surrounding all except the church itself. The only windows to be seen were in the church, and these were stained with images of the apostles so that no one could see in or out. The cloister within held our gardens, where herbs and some vegetables were grown. The buildings around the cloister were vast, all interconnected, so that it sometimes seemed, in those early days when I still lost my way, as though they consisted of no more than series of passages leading one into the other. Because of my family's wealth and importance in the city I was given one of the larger cells. It covered two stories, the upper my main quarters with my chambers and a library, the lower the rooms where I could receive guests, as well as a servants' quarters, though I had none.

Though it often drew consternation from the Abbess and the other Sisters, I read inveterately, whatever I could lay my hands on. In fact, the only acknowledgement from my father that I existed came in the form of the volumes he would send to the convent for me. These were my only conduits to the outside world, of which I had seen so little, confined as I was away from those who might damage my honor. They also provided my only pleasure during those early, solitary years, for, as in my own home, most of those at the convent would have little to do with me. The other Sisters of the Black Veil had heard tales of me and my mother from their families, and they soon spread them to those of the White Veil and even among the servants. I have to admit I did not help matters with my own actions, giving everyone I passed the evil eye and making strange noises and gestures during mass. The more frightened their reactions, the more amused I was, and the more I tried to elicit from them.

In those days, before I had taken the veil, I was constantly called before the Abbess and our Father Superior to explain myself. There were even threats of calling in the Inquisition to investigate certain rumors, which never materialized. Probably they understood I was nothing more than a foolish child, lonely and hurt and without a friend in the world. Or perhaps they were afraid of me and what I might do, I cannot say.

I found my way among them, eventually becoming an accepted, if not beloved, part of that family of Sisters. After my outbursts in those early years, I put myself to the task of living harmoniously with my fellow Sisters, having one heart and one soul seeking God.

And if I was given to despair in certain private moments at what the life that lay before me was, now that I had left the tempests of the profane world, never to return, I did not let it overwhelm me. I tell myself now that I would have stayed among them for all my days had events been allowed to transpire differently, but perhaps that is not true. I have always been given to restlessness and sin.

The deepest sorrow comes from the most profound joy, there can be no other way, and so it was for me in La Encarnación. My friendship with Sister María de Gentileza, and the love I had for her, doomed me to misery when it was ruined. That I played my part in that destruction only cuts the wound deeper, even still, all these years later.

I believe we arrived at the convent near the same month, certainly the same year, though our paths never crossed. She was of the White Veil, those whose duty is service to the monastery, being without a dowry to offer. No doubt she knew of me long before we ever had occasion to speak. Perhaps we even had spoken and I just do not remember doing so; it was often so for me and those beneath my station, unless they did something to attract my attention. And this she did, not long after we had both taken the veil.

I recall the first time I noticed her as we all sat for morning prayers in the nun's choir. We were in the same row, though she was on the other side of the choir with the rest of the Sisters of the White Veil. I had a feeling throughout our prayers of someone watching me and when, at one point, I raised my head from my devotions to look about the choir, I saw another head raised above the sea of bowed veils. Our eyes locked and held for an eternal moment, before we both ducked our heads, returning to our supplications. It was like a tremor through the earth, that shared glance, all the more disorienting because it lasted but a heartbeat.

I caught her at it again that evening, and the next morning too. It became a dance, each of us trying to find a moment when we might risk that stolen glimpse of the other. She had roused in me a hunger I did not know existed, a curiosity beyond my books, to know her, to understand what was behind those looks. Although I say that I had found my way among the other Sisters, I passed my days alone for the most part, as I preferred it. But now here was someone who looked at me not with revulsion or anger, but with a desire to know me, and I found myself hungering for her

7

companionship.

The next days were exhilarating, as our game at prayers continued, but I soon grew tired of it, especially as it became clear the girl did not have the courage to do more than she already was. I have never lacked for courage, and one morning after prayers I engineered a chance meeting between us, in one of the passageways where I knew she would pass by on her way to the infirmary to carry out her morning duties. There was a storeroom of some sort nearby, little used, and I marked my steps to ensure that we met at its door.

She was alone, as I had hoped, and she looked frightened when she came around the corner and saw me waiting for her, as though I had appeared from the very air. Before she had a chance to do anything, I grabbed her by the wrists and pulled her close and then led her, trembling, into the storeroom. With the door closed there was little light, but my eyes have always been keen to the dark and I kept her close so that I might easily see her. She had the face a painter might give to Our Holy Mother or the saints, innocent and beautiful. The look of a generous soul, and that she was.

I slacked my grip on her a bit and then, breaking our vow of daily silence, whispered to her, Sor María, what are your intentions with me?

She would not answer and struggled against me, trying to free herself and flee before she fell further into what she knew was sin. I did not let loose my hands from her wrists, brushing my thumbs against their insides to try to calm her. At last she relented, seeing no other path before her.

I have none, she said, her voice edging with tears.

Then why have you been looking at me during prayers, I asked her.

They say you are too much in your books, that you have no mind to others or to God.

I was taken aback by this. Yes, I told her. They say that and more. Does it bother you?

No, she said, no. It is only that I do not have my letters.

I could see the tears running down her cheeks, and though I longed to brush them away I dared not loosen my grip upon her.

Something like a sob escaped her. I know it is not my place. I know it is disobedient of me and that I should find my happiness in our service to God and the convent.

She could not give voice to the thought, so I did. I will teach you, if you like, I said to her.

She fell to her knees in what I worried was a faint, but she was only weeping, her whole body trembling. I comforted her until she had regained herself and then told her what she should do if she wished to give in to this desire.

That night she did not come, but the next she did. It was well into the evening, when those in the dormitory had mostly settled again for the second sleep. Sister María had gone to the latrine and then not returned, instead coming to my door, which I had left open. As I had told her, if she was careful she would not be noticed, and so it was. I led her to my chambers, not wanting to risk a candle on the main floor, where it might draw the eye of someone passing through the corridor.

I sat her at my writing desk while I leaned over her shoulder, both our faces bathed in the flickering shadows from the candle before us. I had no grammars then, though I would acquire some later, so I simply laid out the book I was reading, showing her the letters and words. I took some paper and a quill and wrote out the alphabet down one side of the page. I could feel her breath on my neck as I did so. Then I bade her to write the letters as I had. She tried, but her hands were shaking so violently the ink was blotted and smeared. I threw the page on the floor and wrote the alphabet again and gave her the quill. This time I put my hand around hers and guided it from the ink well to the page and through each of the letters. By the time we reached the "k" her trembling had subsided, and when we reached the "v" her breath sharpened with excitement, as did mine.

How to describe the months that followed? I cannot do them justice; they were among the happiest I have known. Sister María would come every few nights—more frequently might have aroused suspicions—and I would instruct her in my quarters, our arms intertwined around whichever volume I had pulled from the shelf,. She proved a quick study and showed real skill with her lettering, forming each smooth curve with a delicate care that was splendid to watch.

The more she demonstrated her facility, the more she hungered to learn, and the more I desired to teach her. It was glorious, no doubt. I do not care what you or anyone else might say about it. I will settle my accounts in the afterlife and I know which side of the ledger I will put these days on. Still, I might have given it up had I known what would pass once we were discovered.

I am smiling as I read this over, thinking about what you will say once you have the opportunity to read it. I shall look forward to that; it will ease the drudgery of this task. At least I shall not want for hours and days to complete it.

Sor María was a troubled soul, unfit for life outside the convent. Although I suppose much the same was said of me, both while I was there and after I had left. In her case, the world as it was proved too much to bear, while the world of books, poetry and philosophy and such proved much more amenable. There existence was stable and unmoving, not one thing and then another. I was her opposite in so many ways, always longing for the world beyond where we were kept captive and safe, but we became fast friends in spite of it.

She always feared the moment of our discovery; from our very first time together she foresaw the end. If I am honest I did as well, for it was only a question of time and happenstance before someone stumbled upon our arrangement. In spite of its size, the convent was a small space in the grand scheme of things, and we were not many more than a hundred souls. Any deviation from proper routine would be noticed eventually. But I did not fear discovery. If I am honest, I welcomed it, as strange as that may sound.

Once, when her fears had overcome her, Sister Maria did not call on me for two weeks. She managed, in spite of my best attempts to intercept her in the hallways, to avoid me at every turn. Even during our prayers she would not answer my gaze, never raising her eyes from her obligations. Seeing no other recourse, and not wanting to cease our arrangement, for she had learned so much and we had both enjoyed it so, I took what even then I knew was a rash step. Now it seems madness, but I was young and without care or fear.

I went to the dormitory after everyone had settled back into their beds for the second sleep, to her very cot, and roused her. I moved like a wraith, not disturbing a soul, until I was beside her, where I slipped back her covers and pressed my hand against hers. She started awake with a cry, which I smothered with my other hand. When she had regained herself I released her and then leaned in close to whisper to her: You see, there is nothing to fear. I could tell by the excitement shining in her eyes that her courage had been restored, and I led her from the dormitory to my cell, where we resumed her study.

After that she did not stray from me, and we read through many of the books I had, including some romances that I had managed to smuggle past the Abbess. She had progressed enough that we could read to each other, which we did, whispering so our voices did not carry, both of us pressed against the other that we might share the candlelight and our voices. The days after would be ones of sweet exhaustion, our lack of sleep more than balanced by the pleasure we had taken the night before.

One night our pleasures unseated our senses so much we lost the hour and a new day arrived to find us still together. We could not tell, of course—there were no windows in my cell where we might have looked out to see the first stirrings of the sun before it leapt over the horizon. So we stayed, I spellbound by her whispers as she read the words on the page, she entranced by the words themselves, until the door to my quarters was opened.

Sister María turned white as a ghost, and for a moment I feared she would faint dead away. I was nearly as startled and am embarrassed to say that I directed a curse at the woman standing before us: Catarina María, the maid who cleaned my quarters each morning. The girl seemed almost as frightened to find us together as we were to be discovered, her mestiza colors darkening in the candlelight. Seeing that restored my composure and I acted promptly, sending Sister María on her way to ready herself for morning prayers and then taking my arm around the girl and explaining to her what she had just seen.

It was nothing, I told her. I was helping Sister María write a letter to her sister on a private matter. She did not want the Abbess or anyone to know about what she needed to write, and so she had asked me to be her notary and to send it for her. You understand.

The girl nodded, though she was clearly still suspicious. I seized her by the shoulders and looked her in the eye. The letter is on a very personal matter, naturally, so I must ask that you say nothing of what you have seen to anyone in the convent. Who knows what rumors might be spread, yes? You know how delicate a soul Sister María is. Such a thing would devastate her.

I did not release her until she had given me her word. Her face showed no expression as she said it, her eyes void of emotion, but I was confident I had command of her. She was only a mestiza servant after all, granted leave by the convent to wear the veil. If it came to anything like standing to account before the Abbess or the Father Superior, my word would naturally weigh more than hers. Sister María's would as well. Though she was but a girl, Catarina María was no fool; she would know that as well as I.

The bells rang, calling us for morning prayers, and we left it there for the moment. I knew I would have to do more to keep Catarina María from speaking. We were creatures of the same heart, the two of us, one thing and then another as custom demanded, seizing whatever advantage was offered. We had come to an earlier arrangement where she could come to my rooms to clean them before first prayers, which was what had led to her discovering us. I was often awake anyway, having always preferred the night hours to those of the day, no doubt an inheritance from my mother. The gloom of candlelight has always passed easily for me.

In the days that followed, my confidence proved misplaced. Word travels quickly in a monastery, as you no doubt know only too well, and soon pursuing me down every hall were the veiled looks and whispers of my fellow Sisters. Sister María reported much the same to me and, worse, she was certain that someone had been following her as she went about her daily routines. This gave me pause, for someone was obviously attempting to see if the rumors that Catarina María was spreading were true.

We must take great care this next while, I told her. The Abbess will be after us otherwise.

We had managed a moment alone after our midday repast, when the other sisters were in their cells or the dormitory passing an hour in quiet reflection. Sister María seemed, to my eyes, panicked as though at any moment we might be discovered.

Be silent and nothing will come of it, I tried to reassure her. Gossip will find someone else unhappy given time.

That is easy for you to say, she said to me. Your honor is not at stake.

This was not entirely true—as someone of a higher station I obviously had more to lose should the stories being whispered take more solid form—but there could be no doubt that Sister María cared much more than I about such things. I, as you well know, have never given much credit to these sorts of concerns. They are the worries of the commons and I am not of that stock.

Be silent and do not call on me, I insisted to her. If we leave off a few days the talk will die down, you will see. When the chance presents itself we may meet, but take care.

I left her with those words and the fire of my eyes. If I could not calm her I would at least discourage her from doing anything rash. In my mind there was nothing to worry about, for I had lived with such talk all my life. This sort of womanly chatter did not even penetrate my ears; it was to be expected and never amounted to more than just talk. My greatest fear had been that Catarina María might have spoken to the Abbess or, God forbid, Father Superior Esteban after she had seen us at our lessons. That would have proven a difficult situation to resolve. The fact that all we heard were whispers meant that she had not. It also meant that we could deny all should Father Esteban call us to account.

No, I was quite sure nothing would come of this, provided we could keep our nerve. That proved difficult for Sister María, always a delicate soul. In the ensuing days, as the whispers and stares continued unabated, she slowly began to unravel. Each time I would mark my day's routines to hers, so that we could chance upon each other in one of the monastery's many winding passages, she would not meet my eyes. Once, when we were quite alone in a hallway, with no chance of being overheard, she would not even pause in her step to share a word.

I began to fear she was about to do something foolish, like confess to the Father Superior, and I determined to act before she did. The trick was to find some way to force her to speak with me without drawing the suspicions of the rest of the convent upon us both. It hurt me to see her suffering so, and I knew her guilt, over what she saw as her unnatural urges, would be assailing her mercilessly.

At last I struck upon what I thought was an ingenious solution: I would arrange to meet Sister María—not in secret, far away from the prying eyes of the other sisters, but where all the Viceroyalty might venture upon us. Our convent had a parlor where, as is the custom, we Sisters might receive guests from the forsaken world. These all had to be approved by the Father Superior and the Abbess. Mostly they were relatives, though in my case, as my family had abandoned me to the convent, I had only a friend of my

13

mother's who would come to visit each week.

Her name was Michaela de Malagueña. She had been my mother's one friend in Lima, and she was a source of comfort to me throughout my time in the convent. A true woman. Many times I can recall sitting, restless, in her lap as she and my mother whispered of her life and her sufferings. I do not know how they had come to be acquainted, but I think she may have been a little in my mother's thrall. Many were—my father included, though it drove him to bitterness. Michaela treated me as though I were her daughter, bringing me gifts and helping me when I had need, and for that I have always been grateful.

In this case I asked her to contact one of Sister María's sisters, a simple girl, and have her arrange to visit her sister the next day. Michaela also arranged with the convent's gatekeeper to meet me, and contrived to arrive at the same time as the girl so that the four of us found ourselves side by side in the parlor.

Sister María was agitated, and apologized to her sister and said she could not speak to her, but her sister begged her to listen to me. Michaela, bless her heart, had given the girl a little bit of silver. One of my great regrets in this life is that I have not been able to repay that woman what I owe her for all she did for me and my mother. That is not the only debt I have on my account, as you know only too well.

At last, after many entreaties from both myself and her sister, Sister María relented and stayed, though she would not look at me, staring with pleading eyes at her sister while I smiled and talked and looked at Michaela. It was important that we keep up this act, for Sister Theresa was sitting nearby and it was her duty to listen to all that was said in the parlor, to ensure that we did not fall to temptation and sin. She was an old woman, though, and her hearing was going, something I had discovered during one of Michaela's earlier visits. Michaela had been sitting with her back to the sister, and when I mentioned some gossip from the city she had passed along, Sister Theresa had looked momentarily confused before taking a cue from my grin and chuckling. So long as we kept our voices low and appearances as they were, she would suspect nothing.

I know your heart is troubled, I told Sister María, but you need not worry. That girl is a mestiza. If it is her word against mine before the Father Superior, mine shall carry all the weight.

It does not matter, she said, her voice breaking with emotion. Everyone knows.

You mustn't worry about that. It will pass, as I said. You will see.

Listen to your friend, Maria, her sister said to her, taking her hand. You are a simple girl and not of her breeding.

I smiled my thanks at Michaela for her fine work. Soon you will be able to pass for someone of my breeding, don't forget. Isn't that what you desire?

Yes, María said, and began to weep. Her sister consoled her, and I pretended to converse with Michaela, giving María a few concerned glances for the benefit of Sister Theresa.

It is wrong, though, she said when she had recovered herself. It is a grave sin to be as lustful as I am.

Is it, I wonder? I said to her. If it were up to the Father Superior, none of us would have our letters, and he is a fool.

No, I am unfit before the eyes of God. I must confess and put my soul on the right path.

She began to weep inconsolably then, and this finally drew Sister Theresa to see that everything was all right. María was so beside herself I feared she would confess everything then and there, but she kept her counsel and governed her emotions at last.

When Sister Theresa had gone back to her seat I took Michaela's hand in mine, and told Sister María in earnest: If that is what is in your heart then that is what you must do. But do not act rashly, I beg you. Wait two more days and pray on it. God will show you the true path of your devotion. Let God rule your heart, not the chatter of our sisters. They are as weak and sinful as you and I. Don't let their foolishness lead you to an imprudent act.

To my immense relief, Sister María agreed. I was still convinced that her desire and her dedication to me would win out in the end, provided I could put some end to the gossip, or at least turn it in another direction. That is what led me to my grave and unforgivable error. I was furious, I must admit, though not at María—she was too sweet a soul. I longed so much for things to return to the way they had been, but that is not the way of this world. Alchemists may be able to transmute the elements, but they cannot return them to their native state, for that is always lost in the transmutation. And so it is with us.

I did not understand this at the time and my anger led me to confront Catarina María. I found her that afternoon, after my talk with Sister María, in the cell of one of my neighbors, Sister Rosa. She was an elderly woman, a cousin of Pizarro by marriage it was said, and as a result she had the most lavish quarters in La Encarnación. Catarina María was there mending a pot in the kitchen, for Sor Rosa's cell was so expansive she could have her own meals prepared, and often did, rarely joining us in the refectory. Catarina María was alone, the other servants elsewhere for the moment, and Sister Rosa was upstairs in her quarters—down for a moment's rest, no doubt.

Why are you spreading these tales, I asked her as soon as she had noticed me.

When she had recovered from my sudden appearance, she said: I am not the one lying.

Stop this nonsense, I said. You do not know who you are dealing with.

Why, are you going to use your sorcery on me, she asked, spitting on the floor as she did.

I slapped her, one of my rings breaking the skin on her cheek and drawing blood. Remember your place, girl. And don't forget all that I've done for you.

Seems I was not the only one to be given your favor. This was said with a smirk so insolent I almost struck her again.

Let us go to the Abbess together, then, I told her. We can each lay out our stories and see who she finds has acted ill.

And let you cast a spell on her, as you have already no doubt?

I cannot begin to describe how enraged I was that this ignorant child should act this way towards me, treating me as a common woman of her domain, and repeating the most scurrilous of rumors that had followed me throughout my days in the convent.

Chunchu, I called her. Keep your tongue still.

Will you change into a bird, then? Or change me to some kind of vermin?

I did neither, tearing off her veil and seizing her hair, pulling it so violently her head seemed to go perpendicular with the rest of her body and I was left with a bloody clump of hair in my hand.

I was willing to be forgiving before, you chunchu cur, I said to her as she wept on the floor. I will see you regret your slander.

I stormed away before she had a chance to reply and before Sister Rosa, who had no doubt been roused by our cries, had a chance to investigate.

The bell rings for evening prayers so I must pause my narrative here. Before I leave the ink to dry I should take a moment to reflect. As you unfailingly tell me, this opportunity you have afforded me allows for that. What brought me to such a state and doomed my friendship with Sister María? That I am foul of temper will be of no surprise to you, but it is something which has always launched me headlong into the direst of straits with no heed for consequence. Had I not told Sister María to stay quiet and all would pass? I would not even heed my own words and wisdom, so great is my wrath when my honor and dignity are challenged. I wreak hell on all those who insult me no matter that I too am consumed in the conflagration.

The evening following my confrontation with Catarina María I had a restless sleep alone in my chambers. My mind, so troubled by the events of the day, gave rise to a feverish dream. In it I was asleep in my cell when I was started awake by a strange noise. I called out for Sister María, but she was not there, and so I left my quarters and cell to investigate. There was nothing in the passage outside my cell, the silence of the convent absolute in that moment. By intuition I went to the left, and there around the corner was a darkening of the shadows, indicating the presence of someone.

I called out to whoever was there, but the presence vanished immediately and I took off at a run in pursuit. After passing through an endless number of passages, I came to the cloister, which in my dream consisted of a four hedge mazes, one at each corner of the courtyard, and a fountain at the center. The walls of the convent loomed over the cloister, threatening to cut off the light from the stars and moon. I detected the presence again, near the fountain, and approached cautiously. As I did I found myself transformed into an owl.

I flew out of the cloister, high into the night sky, and passed over the city below. It lay in the same darkness that held the convent, except for one house in a neighborhood where many of the highborn could be found. I alighted on its balcony and then found myself transformed into a man, an *oidor* by my dress, and stepped from the patio into the candlelit room. It proved to be a bedchamber, and my wife María awaited me.

She smiled as she saw me. At last you have returned. You must call a carpenter to repair the baluster.

I inspected the bed and saw that indeed the baluster was broken. I recalled what my young friend Catarina María had told me earlier that evening while we had been in our drinks, about spending an evening with the fairest maiden in all Peru. In that final and ultimate moment together they had broken the baluster of the fine woman's bed.

It was then I knew that María had betrayed me, in both body and soul. I flew into a rage and came at her with my sword, striking off her head with a fearsome blow. The blood sprayed from the wound, marking everything in the room. I did not stop with one blow, though. I kept on, hacking and slashing in a frenzy, until her body was well marked. Then I turned to the baluster and rendered it into kindling.

Laughter from the patio disturbed my slaughter and I turned to see Catarina María, her face still marked by my ring. I took a step toward her, ready to gain my vengeance upon her for her cuckoldry. Before I could act she transformed into a raven and vanished into the night. I cursed her to no avail.

I threw my sword aside and went to find María's head, which rolled under our marriage bed. I pulled it out and spat in her face and then threw it aside. In crawling on the floor, though, I had gotten my clothes so soaked with my wife's blood they were dripping.

I fled the room, leaving a trail of blood in my wake, running from my home to the street, intending to quit Lima for good. Except that I did not find myself on the street, I had somehow returned to the cloister and was standing beside the fountain where I had taken flight. The light was coming into the sky around me, and for a moment I thought I must have dreamed the entire incident. When I looked at my hands I saw the truth, though, for they were stained with blood, as were my cloak and habit.

I stumbled away from the fountain and found myself by one of the cloister walls. A strange thing occurred then. A vine sprang up from the earth from where I had been standing by the fountain, from the very earth where the blood had dripped from clothes. It crawled along the ground, following my path, and then, when it had reached me, began to climb the wall reaching the top, and disappeared. Halfway up the wall, perhaps a little farther, a flower came into bloom. Its petals and stems were yellow and delicate, such a contrast to the vine itself, which was sinewy and marked with spines. I grasped it, ignoring the sting of the needles, and began to climb the wall. By the time I reached the top my hands were soaked in blood anew.

With that I awoke and found my sheets and covers drenched in sweat and my nightgown clinging to my trembling body.

I can hardly bring myself to write of what followed my confrontation with Catarina María. Those terrible days, they unfolded in something like the nightmare I suffered that night. My whole being wants to shy away from staining the page with the foul words this ink must form. I wonder why that would be? After all, there are other horrific episodes to follow this, some of which you are familiar with, no doubt. Why does this one still trouble my soul as the others do not? Why do I still start awake in terror, shivering from the sweat that sticks to me, like those images do to my mind? Was it my youth, the intervening years proving beyond measure that the world is a fearsome and terrible place where so many of our lives are but a fleeting moment?

I was called before the Abbess after morning prayers the next day. One of her servants ushered me into the sitting room, where she received me sitting stiff-backed in a chair, while I was given a stool so that she might look down upon me, as though she were Queen Isabella herself. Her face was severe, her mouth set sternly, and her eyes unmoving. She was not yet old, though her hair had long turned gray. She had only been Abbess of the monastery some five years. Though she had tried everything in her power, after succeeding to the title following Sister Juana María de León Plaza's death, to intimidate me, I had no fear of her and had paid little mind to her actions.

That day, whether it was from my own nerves or something I sensed in her, I thought would be different. I was seized by a tremendous doubt, though I sat at ease on the proffered stool and met her eyes steadily, with none of the humility expected of me.

I have been told some troubling things, the Abbess said. She proceeded to outline the facts, as they had been given to her. I had been consorting with Sister María in a lewd and illicit manner, and had influenced her to defy the rule of the convent and disregard the holy obedience expected of her by teaching her the act of letters. I had drawn Sister María, as humble and obedient a soul as the Abbess had known, into such sin by the casting of spells and the threat of a grave curse upon her and others who had observed us together.

My only reaction to all this was when my color rose after the accusation of spellcraft was made, for I knew what that would mean. The Abbess confirmed my guess.

These are grave and serious acts, if they prove true, she said to me. Neither I, nor Father Esteban, are capable of making judgments in such matters, so we have asked the Inquisition to send someone to investigate these charges.

I protested vociferously, saying that these accusations were without base or merit, and my accusers were, while of good standing in our community, of a lower class. Fortunately, the Abbess agreed with me.

Because we have no proof of these acts, beyond the words given me, and no doubt Father Esteban in confession, I have asked the Inquisition not to arrest you but to come here and interview all those involved. If they feel there is merit to this they can proceed as they will. God have mercy on your soul.

Here fortune smiled upon me, for I would be afforded the opportunity to put my story against my accusers, whoever they might be. Catarina María seemed the most likely culprit, but in truth there were any number of my brethren who, having heard the rumors the mestiza had spread, might have reported them. Perhaps the Abbess herself had heard the whispers and begun her own investigation. She certainly would not have hesitated to seize any opportunity to rid herself of a problem such as myself. Fear had kept so many of them from acting against me until that moment. Here, then, was their opportunity to pit me against a formidable adversary, as implacable as they thought I was.

I have no idea why the Abbess did not simply have the Inquisition arrest me and then carry out their investigation. This is their normal course of action after all, and she would certainly have been in her rights given the nature of the accusations she had received. I would have been kept in the dark as to the nature of the crimes I was accused of and forced to make my confession for any sins I felt were mine. A difficult situation, for the suspicion of the Inquisitors would lead them to believe that anything I said was an admission of guilt of some kind. With an Inquisitor coming to the convent to conduct an open investigation I felt I stood on much firmer ground, given that the only witnesses were of a lesser class, and one a mestiza.

The Inquisitor, one Doctor Don Carlos de Cagarse y Carrión, arrived the next afternoon, after we had finished our meal and were retiring to our cells for contemplation. He was a tall and introspective man, given to silence by nature, and a man of letters, as all the Inquisition men are. An Inquisitor's first inclination is toward skepticism, and Doctor Don Carlos was no exception. When I first met him to give my initial testimony, his gaze was piercing and he studied me as though I were one of Erasmus's proverbs, to be analyzed and countered with sound logic. His mind brooked no superstition or nonsense, and so he doubted any tale of witchcraft or sorcery as a matter of course, which was to my advantage, for my enemies had no proof beyond their own words.

Events had taken an awful turn by that time, for the evening after my interview with the Abbess, Sister María had fallen gravely ill. She was often given to fainting spells, and during evening prayers had succumbed to one, falling dead away in the choir. There was a flurry of consternation among the gathered sisters and not a few glances in my direction, but the doctor who was brought to the infirmary to look at her said it was nothing more than a usual spell and that she would recover.

She did not improve, though, and that night she began to vomit and expel blood. By morning she was so weak she could not even rise from her bed in the infirmary. When I came to see her after morning prayers she was thrashing about in the grip of what seemed a fit, blood running from her nose as she gagged desperately, bringing forth whatever dark matter lay within her. She was muttering to herself—as though in the grip of a fever—words that had no sense to them.

It was terrible to witness, and I blanched at the sight of her, nearly going faint myself. Already there were whispers among the sisters who worked at the infirmary that María was possessed, or that some spell or curse had been put upon her. The talk only grew in the days that followed as her condition worsened, her body swelling at the joints and also around her stomach, which she would clutch at as if she were in the most awful pain.

I refused to leave her care in the hands of any other, changing her bedding and applying damp clothes to wipe away her fevered sweat myself. I often slept by her in the infirmary, the little I did

21

sleep that terrible week, and when I wasn't caring for Sister María I assisted the other sisters in their tasks throughout the infirmary. This earned me some grudging praise from the Abbess.

She is a mere innocent in this after all, I told her, and a dear friend to me.

I did not care what might be said by the other sisters, or by the Abbess, to the Father Superior or the Inquisitor Doctor Don Carlos—my dear María was in grave need and I would not abandon her. It was not an easy task. She would often rave and spit at me, her eyes afire, and then fall back into an unreachable state deep beneath the shadow of the fever that scoured her. The entire infirmary stank of her malady and the sheets and pillows she lay on each day were fouled with blood, vomit and excrement.

Such a terrible way to pass beyond to her reward. It was then I resolved to die quick by blade or ball—anything but the long agony Sister María suffered. That, my friend and keeper, is a promise I intend to keep.

It was at my second interview with Doctor Don Carlos that I was able to provide evidence demonstrating that Catarina María had cast spells upon Sister María. As I explained to the calificador, my dear friend was in no state to be able to denounce what had been done to her, so I felt that I must suffer that burden.

He fixed me with his skeptical eye, studying my eyes carefully. Why did you not bring these denunciations forward in your last testimony, he asked.

I proceeded cautiously, for though the waters appeared calm, I sensed great turbulence beneath his placid exterior. As to that, I said, I am sure you have heard similar things said of me in your interviews. I know how injurious such accusations can be to the well-being of the mind of a woman, especially when one is innocent of the evils imputed, so I was hesitant to do so until I was absolutely certain.

And you are certain now, he said.

I nodded. As you know, Sister María has been vomiting regularly since she took ill. No natural cause has been given for her sudden change in health.

That does not mean there is not one, the Inquisitor said.

No, I allowed, it does not. There is much of the humors that learned doctors do not understand, to say nothing of the mere sisters of this monastery. Nevertheless, when Catarina María came upon Sister María and I the morning I was transcribing the letter for her.

I still have not seen a copy of this letter, Don Carlos said, interrupting me. I spoke with Sister María's sister and she had no knowledge of it, nor of any circumstances involving her sister that would require such discretion.

As I said before, I told him, I destroyed the letter. I was worried it would fall into the wrong hands if I did not take every precaution. Given what has happened, I am glad that I did.

The inquisitor pursed his lips in dissatisfaction and glanced at the notary, who was recording everything I said. I urge you again to disclose the contents of the letter, in spite of your promise to Sister María, he said. It seems likely she will not recover. She will not have the opportunity to decide whether or not it is something she wishes to offer as testimony.

I hesitated a long while, staring at the back of my hands. Very well, I told him, the letter concerned Catarina María. That girl has pursued Sister María for a very long time, though my dear friend has resisted at every turn the attempt to draw her into that abominable sin. Sister María had hidden it for a very long time because she feared Catarina María, for she has an Indian mother and knows some of their maleficios. Ask those who sleep in the dormitory, they will tell you the same.

The tragedy, I continued, was that when Catarina María came upon us she assumed, for what reason I know not, that Sister María and I had been engaging in that sinful act that she so desired. She reacted with such rage and threats that both Sister María and I feared to tell anyone of what had happened. I burned the letter and vowed silence, and kept my vow even when Catarina María began to spread such slander about me. Only now that events have taken such an ill turn has it become clear to me what has happened.

I have proof, I added, of the spells she has been casting. Since Sister María has fallen ill she has vomited and expelled many things.

And these occurred in your presence, he asked me.

Yes, I told him. In my presence she expelled blood and locks of hair through her nostrils. From her mouth rags, tied together, some with locks of hair within them, others with coal. I have them.

I showed him the rags, most of them blue and frayed, all stained

23

with vomit and blood. He studied them all, picking at the string that had tied them, and then looked at the hair and the coal very carefully. He sniffed them as well and winced, for the stench of it all was quite foul. Other than that I saw no reaction from him. He set my evidence aside and returned his gaze to me.

Do you have anything else you wish to add? His tone managed to imply that somehow I must, that to say nothing else was an evasion and a lie.

I resisted the urge to further denounce Catarina María, or to add anything else to the notary's record, which either Don Carlos or my other accusers might use against me in some way. Better to leave it as said and let the truth find its way. I told him no and he gave me my leave and I returned to Sister María's side.

She went to her reward the next morning. I held her hand as she received the last rites. She was no longer herself, raving at me and accusing me of all manner of sin and misdeed, the shadow of the fever having passed entirely over her soul. The last words she said to me that were in any way coherent were of her child, Aña, whom she begged me to care for when she was gone.

Someone must protect her, she said to me. It is an evil world she has been born into. There are foul things walking in it.

I swear it, I told her. It was an easy vow to make—for, of course, there was no child.

Upon your soul if you have one, she demanded of me, pushing herself up from her pillow so that she could look me in the eye. This was the last time we shared a glance, this one so different from our first taken in secret from across the choir. There was not even any recognition in her eyes, though I searched for it. When she fell back to her pillow her eyes became unfocused, the fevered gaze that had taken hold of her that last week returning. It was as though she were already looking into the beyond.

I swear it upon my soul, I whispered to her, but I do not think she could hear me.

It was not long after that she passed on. In the end, in her very last moments upon this broken earth, her beauty returned, that wondrous innocence and purity that had been a part of her in that first moment I had laid eyes upon her, and which death had nearly stolen from her. Whatever had possessed her in those last days relented in its grip and she was free to go to heaven's reward. The shadows that had covered over her eyes lifted as though the sun were rising within her.

Nothing that is pure can stay so in this world of ours. We who are not cannot help but touch it, to try to claim that beauty somehow untainted by life. Time works its inexorable mysteries on us all and all that is left are the befouled and polluted, tainted vessels whose souls have gone to their greater reward. I can only hope it was so for her.

There is little more to tell of my time in La Encarnación. It became a kind of prison, or perhaps its true nature was simply made apparent to me once María was gone. I can already hear what you would say to me: that the convent freed me from the tribulations and tempests that overwhelm our profane realm. There is truth in that, though less than you believe. And no doubt, as you shall see with what is to come, I am not suited for such a life. If ever I was pure, that time is long past and my sin great.

Doctor Don Carlos concluded his investigation following Sister María's death, and Catarina María was imprisoned on my denunciation of spellcraft and the evidence I provided. I do not know the rest of her story, for she was still being questioned by the Inquisitors, having refused to abjure her many errors, when I left the convent. I hope she was able to find the peace God desires for all our souls, though I suspect things will have gone badly for her.

After the terrible events that had befallen us all, no one would speak to me. Those of the White Veil suspected me of malfeasance in my dealings with Catarina María and Sister María, while those of the Black Veil found the whole enterprise too scandalous. That my name had even been rumored as being involved in some way was more than enough for many of them to condemn me. I understand it, of course; those of us of the higher classes have so much more to lose should there be any stain to our honors. Given what had happened, no matter what was truth, lie or rumor, there was no hope for me ever having any standing in that convent. They had put a mask upon me and I would have to wear it .

I fell into a great despair as a result, and for a time was unable to leave my rooms, even for prayers. That, of course, did nothing for my reputation, but I did not care. The whole world seemed black, and I despaired all. I did not light a candle, subsisting again on the gloom of my childhood. My only nourishment came at night, when I would rise after the first sleep and wander the passages without a candle, as María once had. Always I would end up, as in the dream I wrote of, in the cloister, the sky open above me, the moon and stars beckoning and luminous. Sometimes I imagined I could hear the calls of an owl.

It was in these moments of release that I put a misshapen plan into place. When the melancholy at last relinquished its hold on me, I set to work on the necessary arrangements. I could not stay a moment longer in that prison of my soul, where every book in my library and indeed every passage in the convent reminded me of Sister María. It was too much to bear. The Abbess, I felt certain, was marshaling her resources to act against me as well, having left me alone after María's death and Catarina María's arrest by the Inquisition. No, that place would never have rested easily for me, not after what had been done.

One night I rose after first sleep and started my wandering, as was my custom. I kept to my usual path at first, for I was certain that someone had been following me during my evening journeys. One of the Abbess' spies, no doubt. I passed through the cloister and then back into the main convent, where I entered the chapel and knelt in the antechoir as if to pray. I could feel a presence pass by the entrance to the choir, hovering just beyond my seeing had I turned around.

I waited until the sensation had disappeared and then I left the choir. Beside the chapel was the parlor—locked, of course, but I had procured the key using my nimble magic on the doddering Sister Theresa. Moving quickly now, I passed through the parlor to the gatehouse, where I had not set foot since my arrival at the monastery. I had this key as well and stepped out, trembling, into that wider world. For a moment I stood and exulted at the cool river breeze that caressed my cheek, and at the sight of the roads that ran on into the far darkness, before sprinting blindly down the nearest street. I encountered no one and stopped only when I no longer had the breath to continue.

I threw the keys for the convent over the nearest wall. No doubt some nobleman's son found them and assumed his true love was offering the keys to her heart, or whatever such nonsense they believe of women. I took off my habit and threw it over the next wall; I will leave it to your imagination what that son thought upon finding it. He would be wrong, of course, for the world is much stranger than most know.

Beneath it was not my usual inner dress, but the breaches and tunic I had fashioned from some of my other garments. On my feet were boots that Michaela had managed to smuggle in to me the day before in a new writing desk. I had destroyed my previous one in a fit of rage and anguish, the sight of it too unbearable. In my arms were two of the finest books from my library, which I sold at the market the next morning. With the silver from that I was able to purchase a fine hat, befitting any gentleman, and a little food to sate me on my journey.

I had no destination in mind, only a desire to wander, which has carried me on through the years. Even now I yearn to leave, though you have convinced me of the error of my ways, at least in part. This task will have to satisfy, though it is a meager gruel to sup on after the feasts I have tasted. But these are complaints for another day. I am tired and my eyes grow bleary, the darkness no friend to this duty. No doubt you will want to know what led me commit such an evil, abandoning my fellow sisters and abjuring my vows. I can give no other answer but that the world has always beckoned me and I have gone ever further.

THE ACCURSED NECROPOLIS

IT IS WITH some reluctance that I begin again to scratch this poor ink upon the page. When I showed you my first writings, about the terrible events in La Encarnación, you reacted with such an unbecoming fury, demanding that I abjure what I had written and accept your punishment, that I refused to speak or write further with you. Your retribution has been fierce, no doubt, but I have withstood all till now. At last you have put aside the whip and come forth with sweeter blandishments, and so I have determined to relent with my own obstinance and return to the task that you set me as a condition of our peculiar arrangement. I shall endeavor then to meet my bargain even if you have forsaken your part in it.

After I left the convent I knew I had to flee Lima as well. I was sure to be recognized, even dressed as I was, by someone I knew, especially as the Spaniards of the city were certain to be afire with talk of my leaving the confines of the cloister. I decided to make my way inland from Lima, with Cuzco being my vague destination, though what I sought there I do not know. All I knew for certain was the joy at being able to set my foot wherever I so chose. It was all new to me, you understand. I had seen nothing of the world except for my miserable home and the stern walls of the cloister.

I kept to main roads in those early days, not straying to less-traveled places, for I was still unsure of how to make my way in this strange new world. Also, as I had no coin to speak of, I had to work as I went to ensure my belly stayed full. I had no troubles there, for I was warmly received by the Spaniards in every town I came to. That should come as little surprise, for I was educated and my dress indicated I was not one of those impoverished Spaniards who try to pass themselves as hidalgos. No, I was the genuine article.

The only trouble I encountered was in Huancayo, a dreadful sort of town, hardly fit for the Indians who had no doubt passed many generations there. I worked as a squire there for some hidalgo whose father had accompanied Pedro de Valdivia in the conquest of Chile. He had some land on the outskirts of town and he hired me to see to the sheep and Indians he had there. It was terrible work, the Indians, even the ladinos, no better than useless. The result was that I was miserable, and to salve my anguish I would pass my evenings in the taverns or public houses in the company of my fellow Spaniards. There we would drink and gamble until our blood turned vile.

One night in particular I was well in my cups and hard at cards at my friend Don Tomas' house. There was a young man there, perhaps twenty, his face badly scarred by the pox. He gave me quite a rough go in the hands he dealt, and as I grew more and more inebriated I began to suspect he had it out for me. After one hand, where I lost most of the silver I had earned in Huancayo, sick with the realization that I would be condemned to further months in that abominable place, I accused him of being underhanded in his dealing.

He denied it, slamming his fist and overturning the table, accusing me of being a cur. We traded a few more insults and then, though everyone present tried to intervene, we spilled out into the night to cross swords.

It was as poor a display of swordsmanship as I have been a part of, I am sorry to say. Part of it was the darkness we found ourselves obscured in, the rest owed to my sad state of inebriation, coupled with the rage I was consumed with at being wronged by this young scamp. A few of our companions brought out lanterns to give us some guidance, a maelstrom of shouting filling the street as our various companions sought to give us strength. In some ways the flickering glare of the lanterns did more harm than good, for we were sometimes cast in darkness others in half-light. My eyes have always been keen in the dark, but the drink had dimmed them considerably, so I was at no more an advantage than my young rival.

I ran him through, more by accident than design. As his companions attended to his dying cries, some of them shouting curses at me and others rushing to rouse the local corregidor, I retreated within my companion's house and took up all the winnings we had scattered on the floor. Some of my companions cried out at me for doing so, saying I had no cause, but I waved my sword at them in a wild fashion and they kept their distance, unsure of what madness had overtaken me.

None had, of course—I had simply come to the conclusion that my time in that town had come to an end, one that I hoped would not be untimely. A judicious decision as it turned out, for the youth I had just slain proved to be a cousin of the Alcalde. No doubt I would have been strung up in the town square had I stayed. As it was, I fled town that night with only the clothes on my back and a full purse.

When I at last arrived in Cuzco after many tribulations on the road, my purse much lighter than it had been, I found myself at loose ends. I did not know a soul in that fine city, and for most of my first days there I simply wandered the streets, falling into conversation with whatever Spaniards were about. I had employed the same tactic in the other towns I had journeyed to, and as often as not had found my way into some work, but in that great city all avenues seemed to be denied me.

What changed my fortunes for the better was a chance crossing of paths with one Don Juan de Urquiza, a gentleman from Bilbao, whom I recalled from my days living in my father's home. He had been one of my father's closer friends in that time, often calling at our estate, so when I heard his voice as he joked with some other hidalgos, I immediately remembered who he was. I thrust all worry of discovery aside, such was my hunger and desperation, and strode over and introduced myself.

Fortunately, he failed to recognize me—hardly surprising given I had been a child when we had last met. I was vague as to how we had come to meet previously, saying simply that I was a cousin of my father's, new to Cuzco and in need of employment. Hearing that, he embraced me as a son and went straight to a notary, where he wrote for me a letter of introduction and told me to call on a certain Don Tadeo de la Rosa, a merchant who was looking for someone to handle the affairs of one of his shops in the city.

I called on the gentleman that afternoon and soon found myself

33

well employed. For my first task he gave me a mule and charged me to go to Anta, a day's ride away, to oversee the shipment of some goods by mule train. Before I left we together counted out the number of each good to be sent, of which we drew up a list. In Anta I was to oversee the delivery of the goods and have another list drawn up and notarized to confirm that the numbers had not changed on the journey. Upon my return he took the two lists and read over every item to see that I had not cheated him in any manner. This test passed, he brought me on to run his shop, buying me two beautiful suits, one dark and the other vibrantly colored, promising me 600 pesos a year for my work.

Don Tadeo was a Catalan, though not the worse for it. He showed me great kindness after I had proven myself in my work at Anta, inviting me into his home on occasion and embracing me on the street as one would a son. As for my work, he left me with a ledger, where he had written out what I was to charge for each article in his shop, along with two slaves to assist me, and a list of those in Cuzco with whom he had regular dealings and whom he felt were trustworthy. These I was allowed to give credit for anything they might order in the shop. So I worked day by day, following the rules Don Tadeo had set out, taking ready coin for goods, entering it in the ledger, noting the date, the purchaser and the price, and doing the same when I gave credit.

The next months passed peacefully, as great a calm as I have ever known in my turbulent days. It was not to last; such things never do for me. I am always, soon enough, faced with a storm, whether from my own doing or others. You will say the offense is mine—certainly you took offense after the last part of my sorrowful tale—but here that does not stand muster. Here events conspired against me and brought to ruin the tranquil life I had built for myself.

I can hear your words already, the stern look of your brow matching the tone you will take, the distaste with which you will finger the meager parchment on which I scratch. The world does not fit within these walls, though you would like to pretend it is so. One is faced with choices from which no good can come. They do not speak of such things in your philosophies. So be it. Do not think I could not see what was plain on your face when you tried to force me to abjure my supposed sins, or the look in your eyes when you accuse me of all sorts of vileness, which this record will prove to be false. But enough of my bitterness—back to the task you have set me.

My days I have set out for you, and now I shall turn to my evenings, for that is where I encountered all my troubles, which shall come as no surprise. I had some quarters that Don Tadeo had arranged for me, but I spent little time there. The night has always beckoned for me, and I have never wanted much for sleep. Cuzco, of course, was full of young men such as myself, at loose ends and with a little coin, though never enough, so I did not want for companionship anywhere where Spaniards would gather to drink, gamble and bluster.

The talk was where the trouble always began, for invariably, no matter how playful the insults, someone took them at face and daggers or worse were drawn. In most cases nothing came of this beyond some posturing and embarrassment, but every now and then a duel would result and the authorities would be called. I was fortunate in this regard in that the Corregidor was a friend of Don Tadeo's, so I escaped more than a scrape or two thanks to being his man.

My luck did not hold for long; it never does. One hand I am taking trick after trick, the next I find myself holding no trump and am due a fall. I had befriended the secretary of the Bishop of Cuzco, one Don Antonio de Cervantes, a distant relation of that fine writer, the glory of our age. You do not seem the sort to fancy his romances. I, of course, like all those of my station, see myself in his fine work, for better or worse. At any rate, I had befriended the secretary and often found myself invited to his home to gamble.

On one such occasion ten of us gathered, with four or five always at a table in our cards, while the rest mingled about, talking and drinking. Aside from myself and the generous Don Antonio, there was the treasurer Lope de Alcedo and several friends of his, including one strange-looking fellow I had never set eyes upon before. He was dark haired and dark skinned, but with the most piercing blue eyes I have ever seen. I sat at the table most of the night, as was my habit, and acquitted myself well, accumulating a generous pile of reales. Several times, especially as I began to take the treasurer's coin, I caught this stranger gazing at me from the corner of the room when he thought my eyes were on my cards.

I wondered at his interest and, deciding that it could hardly be friendly, I made a great show of getting full in my drink, talking loudly and unsteadily, all the while keeping a careful eye on the man. Fortune stood by me that night and I kept up my winning ways, which led to much dark muttering by Don Lope and the others at the table. This kept on for some time, as we played deep into the night, the others cursing me and their ill luck, the hours growing heavy on everyone's faces.

My mood, which had been as bright as my fellow players' had been foul, turned ugly when, after losing a hand, I reached into my purse to pay into the pot and found it lighter than it had been. Though I had no proof, beyond my own native instinct, I immediately turned and locked eyes with the blue-eyed Stranger. He returned my gaze, the smallest of grins touching his lips. I marveled at his ability to steal up beside me and take the coin from right before my eyes where it sat on the table. Had the others noticed? Unlikely; they were all too consumed with me and their own gloom with the play going against them.

I had no sense of when or how he might have pulled his trick. As I have mentioned to you before, all my senses are very keen, and on this night, though I had been acting quite the drunkard, I had taken only a cup or two of brandy. And yet he had slipped past my guard, stealing right from under my eyes, without my even noticing.

I vowed then, as I paid out my debts and settled into the next hand, that I would not allow him to succeed in his game again. I slipped my dagger out from my belt and kept it in my lap, my left hand clenched around it, within easy reach of my purse on the table before me. And there I kept my eyes, even as I played on through the next hands, never glancing again toward the newcomer, though I knew he was watching me like a falcon studying its prey from afar. I know only too well the charlatan tricks that can be played, the deception of appearances, where one is there and then not there. No fool am I, I recognized a fellow traveler.

When he came next to lighten my purse I was well prepared for him. As he reached out, making a show of passing by the table, I brought my dagger down upon his hand, the blade gouging right through his flesh and lodging itself in the table, trapping the Stranger there. He let out a yell that quietened the room, and I leapt up from chair, snatching my purse from the table, calling him a devil and a thief.

My strategy was poorly thought out, though, for he was a friend of Don Lope, the treasurer, as were most of those there that night. My only friend in the place was our host Don Antonio, and he did not dare risk his friendship with the treasurer over someone as inconsequential as me, a decision I cannot blame him for. He did step forward and plead for peace, to no effect, as Don Lope and his friends drew their rapiers against me.

I drew my blade as well, thinking only of how I might engineer an escape with my vitals intact. Before the mob could come at me, I brought my rapier down upon the Stranger's still-trapped hand, taking off two of his fingers. He snarled at me, more like a beast than a man in that moment, and then pulled my dagger free and came at me with the rest of them. Though I parried furiously, I was unable to stop them from raking me with their blades. I managed to fend them off only enough to allow me to exit the house, and little good it did me, for I was still menaced at all sides by Lope de Alcedo and his companions.

Leave his guts on the street, Don Lope said to his friends, his voice heavy with drink.

I shall still have more stones than the lot of you, I told him with a sneer. You are as unpaved as an Indian village.

This caused a general uproar among the half-dozen or so men brandishing their weapons in the darkness. They were advancing upon me when Don Antonio, Lord bless him, came around the corner with the Alcalde of the city, whom he had roused from his bed at that late hour. That man called a halt to the proceedings and had me arrested, calling on all the others gathered to follow him to give their statements as to what had occurred.

Strangely, the newcomer with the blue eyes was nowhere to be seen among those who trailed behind me and the Alcalde, cursing and muttering at their poor luck in being unable to finish their task. I, of course, was infinitely grateful that they had failed in that, but something else was troubling me. I was certain that the Stranger had come out with the rest of the mob in pursuit of me as I had made my feeble retreat, but at some point in between the ensuing scrum and the arrival of the Alcalde he had vanished. If his fellows had noticed they made no comment on it, either among themselves or to the Alcalde. Where, then, had the man gone, and to what end?

I had plenty of time to dwell on that, for I was thrown into jail, clapped with irons and set in the stock. I passed a cold and miserable night, bleakly pondering the terrible state I now found myself in. The next day the sun rose and with it came my friend Don Antonio, as true a gentleman as one could wish for, and my master Don Tadeo, who spoke with the Alcalde, a man he knew, and had me let out of the stocks and irons. The Alcalde would not free me, though, for the witnesses had all sworn statements against me.

Surprisingly, no mention was made of the Stranger, the harm that had come to him, or the theft that had precipitated all the events. It was as though he had never been present. I protested to the Alcalde that I wished to press charges against this man, but he waved me away. Neither Don Antonio nor I knew the man's name and the Alcalde had not seen him when he'd come upon the scene, so for all intents and purposes he did not exist. The charges against me had nothing to do with the Stranger. It seems that in the scuffle that had broken out I had, while making my frantic defense, landed a blow on the face of one Mendo de Quinones, which required some seven stitches.

As they were unable to secure my release, in spite of their many and considered pleas to the Alcalde, both Don Tadeo and Don Antonio left me to my fate in the jail, promising to return with what help they could muster. In spite of their cheerful bravado at our parting, I knew my situation was bleak. Neither of my friends had the standing that Lope de Alcedo did in Cuzco and that, combined with the fact that all the witnesses spoke against me, meant I was almost certain to be facing a stiff penalty—no doubt a few years with the army in Chile, battling the savages that roam there.

So began my first spell of imprisonment, though it would not be my last. At the time, the specter of unending days lying before me, filled with poor food and miserable conditions, as the case ran through its gauntlet of appeals, left me in a state of dread and despair. Those nights did not pass easily. Neither do these nights before me now, though I have had ample time to grow accustomed to them.

The case ran its course, with the usual pleas and demurrals. I shall not belabor my narrative with them, for you will no doubt be familiar with the procedures, and little remarkable occurred. As it was clear that I should lose the case, and as he was desperate to keep so valuable a servant, Don Tadeo endeavored to find some means to have the charges against me dismissed. The Alcalde would not hear reason, being a friend of Don Lope's, so Don Tadeo turned to other means, and these he presented to me one month into my incarceration.

Don Tadeo had for some months—since before I knew him, at any rate—been carrying on with a respectable woman, one Doña Beatriz de Guajira. This young woman, already a widow, was the niece of Mendo de Quinones, whom I had wronged. To set things to right with Don Mendo, he proposed that I marry Doña Beatriz in return for Don Mendo dropping the charge against me. It seemed a proper solution to the matter, for I would give this woman a proper husband and end any further bitterness between myself and Don Lope and his friends. For Don Tadeo a better result could not be found: he would be able to keep me for his business and Doña Beatriz for his pleasure.

I refused. I will not be a brother starling in your nest, I told him, while he sought to convince me otherwise.

But there is no hope for a happy outcome to your case, he insisted to me.

We shall see, I said. I shall trust my fate to Our Lord.

He tried for some time to argue otherwise, but I would hear none of it. My faith was proven when some days later Mendo de Quinones was found murdered. The circumstances under which he had been killed were quite mysterious. Some assassin had crept into the bedchamber where he was sleeping with his wife and had slashed his throat and left him there to bleed out, escaping without waking any of the servants or slaves in the house. A remarkable occurrence, it must be said. When the next night Don Ordofto de Aguila, one of the witnesses who had spoken against me in court, suffered the same gruesome fate, all the others, including Don Lope, recanted their testimony and I was set free.

Don Tadeo was ecstatic beyond words at this development. He reported to me that all who had spoken against me now spent their nights in fearful sleep. Those who could afford to had hired guards to stand watch over their bedchambers to see that no one entered, while Don Lope, it was said, was unable to sleep, and spent his nights pacing from room to room in his estate. Given the strange nature of the murders, they all feared that this was not some man exacting vengeance upon them, but a devil come to visit them that no man could stand against.

Though they had no proof—indeed, how could they, for I had been imprisoned while the events in question took place—they felt that I had somehow summoned this blood demon upon them. A ridiculous notion. When they called on the Inquisition to investigate, saying that I had cursed them from my cell and had threatened that they should withdraw their testimony and the charges or die, I was forced to withstand yet further interviews, this time before an officer of the Inquisition resident in Cuzco. Nothing came of this, of course, for there was no earthly proof that I had been involved in those terrible deaths.

So it was that after three months of imprisonment, trials and inquisitorial investigations I came to return to my employment for Don Tadeo in his shop in Cuzco. Happy I was to be able to do so. The only change was that I kept a close eye about me as I wandered the streets, for if Don Lope and his friends still felt that I had worked some sorcery against them there was every chance that they would try to seek justice for their dead comrades. I was careful as well in where I chose to pass my evenings, gambling only with those I knew well and in places where I felt secure. Whether it was due to my caution or the fear of my enemies, I saw no sign of trouble in the months that followed.

The placidity of my days was only marred when, one morning, Don Tadeo arrived at the shop, bringing my father in his wake. Imagine my feelings upon seeing him! How to describe it. I was certain my father would see me for who I was. How could he not, after all? He did not, though he looked me directly in the eye as Don Tadeo introduced us. I felt elated beyond words at that moment, for I had won the trick indeed. If my own father was unable recognize me, then who in creation would? I was no different than the fantastic chameleon, that lizard which can don the mask of its surroundings. I too can disappear before your very eyes.

My elation soon dissipated, to be replaced by rage that this man who, whatever else he had been, was my father, did not know me. Part of me—a very small part, granted—wanted to stand before him and let him know that here was the daughter that had so ruined his honor. Good sense ruled the day in the end, and I walked with my father as Don Tadeo showed him about the shop. I must say, in his defense, that he had every reason not to recognize me. After all, I had been little more than a child the last he had seen of me, and that nearly ten years ago. Now that I was before him I was a different person entirely.

I said little as Don Tadeo regaled my father with tales of his business acumen and success. And, it must be said, with praise for me, his newest servant. I was a natural in all matters business and would be a fine match for any marriageable daughters he might have. I watched my father's face closely at Don Tadeo's words, but he showed no trace of emotion, merely smiling in a friendly way one does when entertaining a friend. They talked some more and then took their leave, Don Tadeo inviting me to join them for dinner that evening at his home. I demurred, saying I had other matters to attend to, not wanting to take the chance that more time spent in his company might cause my father to recognize me.

That was the last I saw of him or any of my family. The moment did not have any of the finality that implies. I felt only a flooding sense of relief when they had gone, the worry and boil of emotion that I had kept at bay at last coming loose. The color rushed back to my face and my breathing steadied. How the two of them had failed to notice I do not know, for I must have looked very unnatural indeed. I have learned a little of what has become of my father in the years since then. He continues to prosper, as he would, for he was always astute in his dealings, and he has seen that his daughters are well matched.

The last I was told was that he had remarried. Enough time has now passed, and since I have not emerged to cause him further scandal and embarrassment, that both my mother and I have been forgotten more or less in the memories of those who matter in Lima. It will be as if we never were at all.

Things began to go poorly between Don Tadeo and his mistress Doña Beatriz in the months that followed my release from jail, and I found myself caught betwixt them. The problem was simply that he was weak and she willful. Their difficulties evidenced themselves to me when Don Tadeo started to spend more time around the shop. Up to that point he had hardly darkened the doorway of his establishment, happy to let me handle its affairs. I must admit I began to worry that he suspected me of some malfeasance with the way that he puttered about, having nothing to do but watch me go about my tasks.

Instead, he began to relate his various tales of woe to me about the hardships he was now suffering with his mistress. It seemed she was unhappy with the way in which he was keeping her, forever asking him to buy her trinkets and jewelry. He had procured her some quarters not far from the shop so that he might have a readymade reason for being in this neighborhood of Cuzco, far from his home with his wife. Doña Beatriz found her home and the surrounding environs unbefitting a woman of esteem and nobility, and pestered him endlessly to find her something in a better part of town.

A man of strength would have handled this easily, cuffing Doña Beatriz about the ears and telling her to mind her station. What was she, after all, but a concubine, Spanish blood or not? Don Tadeo did not have that in him, as I discovered to my sorrow, and, instead of confronting her as a man should, he hid in his shop, where she rarely came for fear of causing a scandal. Instead I was dispatched to tell her that he would not be calling on her that day. There were tears and much hopeless mewling after I delivered Don Tadeo's missives, which I had to ignore, though my instinct was to show her the backside of my sword. A taste of the metal would bring her to her senses, I reasoned. Good sense prevailed, though I was tested.

When she saw that her anguish and emotion had no effect upon me, as they clearly did on Don Tadeo, Beatriz implemented a new strategy, one which I could not resist, for my master found it to his liking as well. I became their go-between, a carrier of messages those days when they were not on speaking terms. Don Tadeo would come to linger around the shop, having nothing else to do but wanting to avoid her, and send me off to give Doña Beatriz the news. I would be received not with tears and anguish, but with a note that I was to carry off to my master. He, after reading it, would wander about in a state of maudlin indecision and then scratch off some note of his own and send me to deliver it.

A more infuriating existence I cannot imagine. What else could I do? He was my master, after all, and I was indebted to him for the help he had given me during my time in jail. I could not very well insult and deny his mistress either, for though he had grown tired of her and spent little time in her company, he had also done nothing to rid himself of her. And I knew her kind well. She would not hesitate to reveal any slight or misstep I made in her presence if she thought it would improve her relations with Don Tadeo. She already thought my master was over-fond of me and that our friendship, and my refusal to marry her, were the cause of her failing relations with him. A feeling she never hesitated to share with me when I called upon her with the latest disappointing news from him.

Events came to a pass one fine spring day when Doña Beatriz, having worked herself into a lather of rage and bitterness, ventured down from her apartment to the shop after I had brought word that Don Tadeo would not be calling on her that evening. She stormed in, her lovely face clouded by fury, seizing me by the arm and demanding to see her lover. Here a man of sterner constitution would have answered duty's call and come forth and dealt with his recalcitrant mistress, but Don Tadeo was formed of weaker matter. He remained hidden in the back while I dealt with Doña Beatriz, telling her that he was not there and that she should return to home, lest she bring doubt to her virtue with her display.

This only served to incense her further. She spat on the floor and declared to me: You speak of virtue and honor. Whose honor is at stake here? Mine alone. I am Spaniard and I should not be treated as though I am some mere Indian harlot.

I tried sympathy then, telling her that I agreed that Don Tadeo was treating her poorly after all the things she had done for him, agreeing to marry me among them. It had no effect upon her, except to send her into further paroxysms of rage. She stamped her foot and struck me in the face, cursing me as she did so.

He has done more for you than he has ever done for me, she said to me. It is enough to make one wonder what unnatural sins occur in this shop.

Here I decided that I had suffered her emotions enough, and that if Don Tadeo was unwilling to deal with her as he should, then I would take matters into hand whether either of them liked it or not. I seized her by the wrist and silenced her with a fierce glare. Her face lost its color and she trembled in fright.

If it were up to me, I told her, you would be tasting the back of my sword. As it is not, I'll simply escort you home, but do not try my patience again, for it is fraying rapidly.

She did not speak after that and I led her from the shop, never

43

relinquishing my grip on her wrist, though she winced from the pain of it. When we arrived at her building I led her up to her quarters and fairly threw her in once she had unlocked the door, telling her that she was not to come back to the shop again.

That is not your place, I told her firmly, and gave her another glare that made her cower.

She nodded and looked demure for a moment, but then changed her tact again, stepping and seizing my hands in hers, looking at me with coquettish eyes. It is a pity that you refused to be married to me, she said to me, you are a man in truth, unlike Don Tadeo. He is afraid to see me on the streets.

I shook myself free of her grasp and made to go, but she soon had me in her embrace again, caressing me freely and cooing in my ear whatever sweet and enticing things flitted into her head. I resisted, for I did not want to make a cuckold of Don Tadeo, though in truth he was little better with the way he let her carry on. After some time I broke free and pushed her to the floor, stamping my foot in frustration.

Do not lower yourself so with me, I said to her. I will not cause Don Tadeo to wear the horns.

He has them already, she said, tears in her voice. No matter what you do, he will have them.

I chose to ignore her and was almost out the door when she called out from where she lay: You act the man, but you are no more man than I.

Bite your tongue, I said, wheeling around and reaching for my rapier.

Prove yourself, then, she said, showing no fear now. Prove you are the man you speak about. Do not deny me your pleasure.

I did not, not that day or the ones that followed.

I often wonder what I gain in this task by telling you the truth of my exploits. It seems to me there is only heartache in it for me, from having to relive all these terrible events anew. The benefit of hindsight does not make it any easier, for look at where I now find myself, condemned to my past, having no future. To say nothing of the heartache that will follow once you have opportunity to read my words again. It was only my perseverance in the face of your punishment that at last spared me from your cruel actions after you read the first part of my tale. What will the truth gain me now but more pain and misery? Perhaps I would do better to tell you what you would most like to hear, yet I cannot, for in all things I must answer to Our Lord.

I have much to answer for in my dealings with Don Tadeo, as you will not fail to note when you read these words. After all he had done for me: giving me respectable employment, taking me under his wing and helping me after my arrest, though it cost him in his standing with those of influence in Cuzco. I could not hope to repay all that he had done for me, so instead I betrayed him, left him wearing the horns, all for a nefarious-hearted woman. Yet even though I knew she was devious, and that my time with her could only poison my relationship with my master, I could not stop myself.

Day after day I called upon Doña Beatriz when I knew Don Tadeo was with his family or away from Cuzco. I often swore that I would not, my guilt at what I was doing working at my conscience, but my senses would soon overwhelm me and I invariably found myself locking the shop and making my way down her street. She urged me on with her caresses and the sweetened words that would pass from her lips, telling me that I was twice the man Don Tadeo was and gave her double the pleasure.

One of the consequences of my affair with Doña Beatriz was that she ceased in her complaints to Don Tadeo, no longer insisting that he attend to her at every moment or provide her with all that she desired. As a result he began to take a renewed interest in her, for it was only her incessant demands that had driven him away. She was, after all, a very comely woman, with bright eyes and an insouciant smile that, in combination with a tongue that never stayed still for long, were enough to make any man take leave of his higher senses. Don Tadeo's resumption of his affair with Doña Beatriz posed certain obvious problems for me. I was forced to close the shop some afternoons and hope he did not chance by in order to find some time with the lady who, though she was now seeing two gentleman, had an ardor that showed no abatement.

The days passed for me in alternating states, of delight and rapture on the hand, and consternation and regret on the other. Adding to my doubts was the lady herself, who began to admonish me with the same complaints she had once uttered to Don Tadeo. She wanted me to lavish her with gifts of clothes and the accouterments of a respectable lady of standing. None of this I could afford, as I never failed to tell her sternly, putting a growl into my voice. She had lost all fear of me, though, and our time together became one of ceaseless complaint on her part.

One day, when her entreaties had yet again failed to move me, she suggested that I steal from Don Tadeo if I was in such a state of poverty. I slapped her and told her to put such thoughts from her mind, that I would not betray Don Tadeo any more than I already had. She moped about in a state of dejection for the rest of our time together that day, hardly giving me a glance, let alone a word from her sweet tongue.

The next time we met she had recovered her spirits and was loving and joyful. Her light mood did not last, though, and soon she was at me again, demanding that I steal from my master. I flew into a rage. I had my blade drawn, and but for the door to her bedchamber, which she quickly threw closed and barred, I would have been upon her. After I had finished raging at her, stomping my foot and kicking at the door, which did not yield an inch, I sat before it and listened as she told me in her sweet voice what she had in mind.

You think he is kindness itself, she said of my master, but I know he is as conniving as you or I.

This I did not believe, and I would have stormed against her firm door again, but she had already begun to whisper her astounding tale to me. It seemed there was a conquistador, Esteban Eguiño de Córdoba, one of Pedro de Valdivia's lieutenants during his time in Chile, who had come into some treasure—where and how, Doña Beatriz could not say. I had thought Chile a barren land of desert and savages, but no matter. Not wanting to share it with his fellows, he hid it, bringing it back with him to Cuzco when his service was done.

Here he remained through the years, hardly spending a reale of the riches by all accounts, and some years later he made the acquaintance of Don Tadeo. One night, when they were heavy into cards and brandy, Don Esteban began to lose poorly and suffer the taunts of his fellow players, as happens when drink has been flowing easily. He did not accept it with grace; instead he ranted at them all of the great wealth he had in his secret possession—gold and treasure that would make any man among them weep. Such bold claims, of course, caught the attention of all those gathered, and many veiled looks were exchanged.

This she told me in such a hushed voice that I had to lean my ear against the door to hear it plain. I could smell her, perfumed and oiled as she always was, on the other side of the door, could almost imagine her leaning as close to it as I was forced to.

Now you will tell me that Don Tadeo stole it, I said to her.

That he did, Doña Beatriz said. But whether from guilt or fear he has not spent a coin of it, and will not until Don Esteban is well and buried.

And how did you come to know of this, I asked her, the disbelief plain in my voice.

He told me, she said, and here I could almost imagine her warm breath upon my ear. Do not underestimate my powers. I have the key to unlock the door to any man's heart.

Of that I am sure, I said. I do not see how this changes anything.

When she spoke next she had leaned away from the door, her voice distant and frustrated. Is it not as plain as your face? If you were to steal it from him. he could not very well accuse you of theft while Don Esteban is alive. It would only mark his own guilt.

I considered this a moment. There is sense there, I admit. But what if it is in fact treasure, some golden idol that the Incas kept? Do we not mark our theft, then, with Don Esteban?

That is a simple matter, she said. Leave that tale to me. Women know how to spin such tales that men lose the trail and wander lost in the wilds never to find home again.

That I do believe, I told her. That I do believe.

When I asked her where the treasure was she said she did not know, only that Don Tadeo had told her it was easily at hand, should he require it. Evidently he had promised her the wealth once the conquistador died, but she had come to doubt his words in the past months when her complaining had turned him from her. So now she came to me. I was to ascertain the location of the fortune and steal it, presumably while she kept my master distracted. We would share in the spoils; she promised me marriage, in fact, a life of delight and luxury such as neither of us had ever known.

I swore to her I would think on the matter, and she urged me not to delay, for according to her Don Esteban was not in good health and once he was gone our chance to escape without justice disappeared too. I went on my way then, my heart troubled by the emotions warring within it. The days that followed would not be any easier.

Before you accuse me of all manner of crimes, which no doubt you will do regardless of what I write here—you see I have seen through your disguise—I must insist that I did not give much consideration to what Doña Beatriz had asked of me. She was a reptile masked in female dress. I did not believe for an instant her tale of the stolen conquistador treasure; it was too fantastic by half. If Don Tadeo had a hidden fortune, an idea which I was not yet sure whether I gave any credence to, then I thought it far more likely that he had gained it here in Cuzco through some nefarious means, which no doubt explained his circumspection with spending it.

I suspected as well that the treasure would prove considerably more difficult to acquire than she had intimated. Don Tadeo was no fool, after all; he would not simply leave the treasure unguarded. So I thought on it a bit, but did nothing to ally myself with Doña Beatriz in seizing it. I had little need of treasure at that moment— my belly was full and I had a good master and the opportunity to wander wherever I should so choose.

All that changed one terrible and harrowing evening, which I shudder even now to recount. Look at how my hand shakes; you shall hardly be able to make sense of these scratchings, and perhaps that is best. Some things should be left for the darkness to hold.

The night in question was perhaps a fortnight after Doña Beatriz had unveiled her proposal to me. In the time since I had stalled and prevaricated, frustrating her to no end with my refusal to give her a clear answer. To ease my mind of all the troubles that had wearied it in past weeks, I decided to pass the evening in cards and drinking at one of my usual haunts. I had stayed away these past months out of fear of reprisals for what had transpired with Don Lope and his friends, but I judged that enough time had passed for passions to have cooled somewhat. Had they wanted to seek their revenge against me there had been ample opportunity before this night, or so I believed. How foolish I was.

The hours passed easily, as they always do when I am at my cards. I hardly looked up from the table, and after some poor hands to start the game I began to add to my purse, sending many players out to the embrace of the cold evening, their hands empty and their hearts clouded with anger. Did one of these men know me? Or was it someone else who recognized me and went to find those who had a vendetta against me? It matters little; all that I know is that as the evening drew to a close, I, flushed with brandy and my success, raised my eyes from my cards to see the blue-eyed Stranger sitting down across from me.

This gave my heart quite a stop, but I kept my composure as best I could, even as he smiled a coldblooded smile at me. I gave him the most insolent smirk I could muster, but it disappeared when I saw the hand that I had wounded in our earlier confrontation. There was an ugly scar where I had plunged my dagger in, pinning him to the table momentarily, but the fingers that I could remember taking from him with my vicious blow were whole and unmarked. Though seeing it unsteadied me greatly, I gestured at his hand and said to him: You appear to be marked as a thief.

He smiled thinly in turn, his eyes narrowing and a bit of a flush creeping into his face. It is a reminder, he told me, of a coward and things still to be done.

We played some hands, most of our fellow players abandoning us to our fates, until there were only two left besides ourselves. Fortune continued to smile on me and I won, effortlessly it seemed, taking the Stranger's coin and causing a terrible redness to discolor his face. He began to mutter to himself, words I could not quite make out, and when his hands were idle the one found the other, touching at the digits that I was certain I had removed, as if to check that they were still attached.

At last, as I continued to take his silver and taunt him for his lack of ability, the Stranger could stand no more and he stood up, throwing his chair aside, and reached across the table to grasp me by the collar with the very hand that I had marked. You are nothing but a gamester and a carpet-monger, he shouted at me, and threw me to the floor.

I was at my feet in an instant and had my rapier drawn, as did he. I am no coward, I said to him. My rapier will stand the same as any other man's.

That I would see, he said to me with a laugh. I know a capon when I see one. I would hear your castrato's voice now.

He came at me, drawing blood on my arm with a quick feint that I was unable to parry. I cursed and launched a rage-filled assault that he easily turned aside.

I am no eunuch, I said to him, spitting on his boots as I did so. I am no sentinel-watcher. Look at my master if you doubt it, for he wears the horns and I am the cause.

If that be so, he said, then I shall see that the stones that give you all your pleasure, and your master such grief, be cut off. You'll be free of this fleshly life and can get yourself to a cloister.

He came at me again with his sword and we did battle for a time, each of us drawing blood but neither landing a telling blow, until at last several of our fellows interceded, calling for good sense and reason to take hold. The owner of the establishment came down from upstairs, where he had been seeing to his women, and threatened to call the Alcalde if we did not leave the premises, and so we did, each of us going our separate ways into the inky blackness of the night.

I knew that this was but a temporary suspension in our hostilities and that the flag of truce would not last, even though we had gone in opposite directions. I am not ashamed to say that I fled at a run, for the Stranger had proven himself to be a skilled with the sword and of prodigious strength. I much preferred to meet him on ground of my own choosing, where I could bring certain advantages of my own to bear. This night, I knew, was no time for that, and so I tried to make my way home as quickly as I could. I did not take a straight route, ducking and dodging down streets, for I feared he might know where I lived and try to intercept me.

My path took me through a cemetery, formerly a heathen burial ground now consecrated to Our Lord. There are many tales of what can befall the wayward soul who wanders into a necropolis in the dead of night, as I did that evening—and little wonder, for there are only foul reasons to be about at that time and in that place, and few take kindly to discovery. I have always been at ease with the night, as I have told you many times, and the dead do not worry me. I shall join them soon enough. But that evening I erred grievously, for the necropolis I ventured across was accursed, unbeknownst to me, and I was to see the face of the devil himself before the night was through.

When I had passed through the cemetery gates I headed for the higher ground, where the wealthy families of Cuzco were interred. Their ostentatious mausoleums, as large in some cases as a pauper's home, populated the knoll near the center of the burial ground. Here I secreted myself so that I had a clear view of the gates and road beyond and could see if the Stranger was still in pursuit of me. I was quite certain he was, for at various moments, when I had paused on my circuitous route home, I had been overwhelmed with the distinct sensation of someone watching me from the deepest shadows that even I could not peer into. The hair had stood on my arms and neck, and I even thought I smelled something on the cold air, rank and vile.

I waited, pressed against the hard ground, the cold of the mountains leeching into my bones, the only sound my own soft breathing. No one passed through the gates, not a soul stirred anywhere within the confines of that place, the dead all at rest. At last, satisfied that I had not been followed, I stood and made to go on my way. As I did, the door to the tomb I had hidden myself behind was flung open and, before I even had a chance to shout in fright, I was seized and dragged into its depths.

The darkness there was absolute; not even the starlight above reached within through the open crypt door. I had fallen hard against some stone, perhaps one of the resting spots within the tomb. My leg had gone numb from it so that I could not even get to my feet, which I knew I had to do immediately, for I was not alone. There was no sound, but a darkening of the shadow told me that whatever had seized me was before me. When I saw this I lunged clumsily at it with my rapier from where I lay on the ground. My blade cut nothing but air. A blow landed on wrist, sending my sword clattering to the stone and leaving me with only my dagger to defend myself.

At last, and I know not how, for there was no light in that infernal chamber, I saw the glint of the devil's eyes through the darkness. They were blue. He emitted a hissing sort of chuckle, unlike anything I have heard before. It was a sound not entirely human, and it chilled my blood. I felt his blade against my throat.

Now, he said to me, I have you at my leisure, carpet-monger.

If it's your coin you want, you can have it, I told him, trying to keep the fear from my voice.

Your voice trembles like a woman's, he said in reply. It is not coin I seek. I'll need repayment for the mark you left on me, and I require payment in kind.

I swallowed and tried again to sound bold: You do not seem to be lacking much there, at least not as I remember.

The Stranger laughed and then struck a match and lit a candle, his blade never straying from my throat. This is what I saw, though I hesitate to put such words to the page, for they are most unholy. Behind him were the stairs I had fallen down leading to the tomb's door, while we were in a small chamber where several skeletons lay in their final repose, still wearing the dress they had been buried in. There was another set of stairs leading below, no doubt to the further remains. All as I had imagined, more or less. Beside me, however, lay a mummy, finely dressed in the Indian style and with a sackcloth about its neck. When I glanced down, and I have no idea what compelled me to do so, I saw that its right hand was missing three of its fingers.

I looked at the Stranger in horror, and he laughed and removed the sword from my neck so that he could wiggle his fingers before my eyes. His taunting afforded me my chance, however, and I got to my feet, leaping at him, my dagger in hand. I caught him by surprise, knocking his sword from him before he could recover. We struggled together arm in arm and, though he had a fearsome strength, I managed to land a blow, my dagger sinking into his gut. But it had no effect on the devil, except to send him into a further paroxysm of rage, and he threw me back to the ground. I landed in the mutilated arms of the dead heathen, breaking him in two, and knocking over a cup, which I had not noticed before, set beside the mummy as though in offering. It was covered in strange runes, the likes of which I had never seen, and the Stranger let out a cry when he saw what had occurred. After a moment I saw why, for the blood within it had spilled out on the stone.

What foul magick is this, I said to him, making a warding sign against all evil as I did so.

Do not play the fool with me, he said, reaching across to pick up the cup and then offering it to me as though we might share a drink. I was motionless, staring at him in horror as he drank what remained and then set it aside.

I know what you are, he said to me. Do not think otherwise. You cannot pull your mask over me.

Again I said nothing, watching his every move and waiting for another moment when I might have the opportunity to strike. My dagger lay beneath me, entangled within the mummified bones of the heathen. I did not know what foul ritual he had planned for me, but I had no intention of seeing it through to the end. I would strike at him when the opportunity presented itself and gain my freedom, or perish in the act. After my failed first attempt he was much more on his guard. In spite of the easy, spiteful tone in his voice, his eyes never left me, even the slightest tremor drawing a sharp look.

He taunted me some more, calling me all manner of things, but I stayed silent and at last he grew tired of this game. With his marked hand he reached down to his belt and pulled out a dagger, the very one that I had branded him with.

Recognize this, do you, he said with a smile, waving it before his eyes.

He put the dagger between his teeth and was atop me before I even realized he had moved, pinning my arms beneath me. I struggled mightily, but it was no use—I was trapped. The only saving grace afforded me was that my left hand was atop the hilt of my dagger, so if I could manage to get my hand free I would have a chance to land a blow. That seemed unlikely, though, for his strength was overwhelming, and his weight did not allow me to move at all. My nose was filled with the smell of dust and bone from the shattered mummy and the rank stench of the Stranger himself, his breath heavy with blood.

Having rendered me helpless, he transferred the dagger to his hand and with great skill opened my neck, setting a steady stream of blood going. This he drank at for a long while, and I could feel myself weakening, my head going light. It was a struggle to keep my eyes open. When he had drank his fill he raised his head and said, laughter in his voice: Now we shall see what sort of stones you have, capon.

He defiled me body and soul. I cannot write more than this. The only reason I am here to write this to you today is that in his urgency he loosed the pressure on my arms for just a moment, long enough that I was able to find the dagger beneath me and take it and plunge it into his neck. My hand did not have the surgeon's skill that his did, I was like a butcher bleeding a pig, but I achieved the effect I sought. The Stranger gasped and his eyes went glassy and his body inert as the blood drained from him. I struggled free of his grasp and fled the tomb and the necropolis, running as fast as I could, though I was badly weakened, until I was home and safe.

What a terrible world we live in, you cannot even know. There are things beyond your imagining, beyond your teaching—though I suspect you know something of them, much as you pretend otherwise. Still, you suppose I am capable of all manner of evil and deviltry, but there is much out there that is beyond whatever you might fathom in its vileness. Such a man was the Stranger, may the eternal fires of hell consume him.

After the events of that harrowing evening I knew I could not remain in Cuzco. Who was to say what Don Lope and his friends might do when they discovered what had befallen the Stranger, for I had no doubt that they would. He was their master, this I knew in my bones; they would do his bidding. That they would blame me I did not doubt as well, for they considered me to be the same sort of devil as the Stranger and capable of all sorts of evil. Never mind that I was a man as they were, I knew they would not relent. The Inquisition would be upon me again, or worse.

And so, though it pained me greatly, I determined to steal Don Tadeo's treasure as Doña Beatriz had asked me to. Since she had told me of its existence I had thought on where my master might have hidden it, and believed I had solved that riddle. It was an easy one to reason, for my master did not have much property in Cuzco where he could hide his riches—only his estate, the shop where I worked and the quarters where I lived. And Doña Beatriz' quarters, of course. This was where I was certain he had hidden them. If he were as fearful of the discovery of his theft as he appeared, then he would not want the treasure stored in those places most associated with him: his home and his shop. Doña Beatriz' seemed the safer of the two remaining places, if only because he could be assured that she would be too incurious and unintelligent to discover its presence.

It took me most of the next day to recover from my struggle with the Stranger. Even still, I was weak and pale when I called on Doña Beatriz that evening. She received me with a show of great concern for how I looked, but I brushed her aside and began my search for the treasure. I went from room to room, tapping at each wall, ceiling and floor until at last, near her hearth, I heard the hollow sound I was looking for. I pried at the stone with my hands, working it free, revealing a hidden crevice, within which I could see the shadow of a chest. When I had taken the hearth apart enough we dragged the chest out and I pried it open, revealing a splendor beyond any I have every seen.

Looking it over, I could see why Don Tadeo had been reluctant to spend the riches there. It gave me pause as well, for the chest was not filled with Incan silver and relics, as Doña Beatriz' tale had made it out to be, but with Spanish reales. Whoever Don Tadeo had taken it from, at one point it had belonged to the Crown. Perhaps a ship had wrecked and he had salvaged this from it, but that seemed hard to credit. At any rate, this much coin could only draw suspicion if it were shown around, so I knew that I would need to proceed with the greatest of care.

Doña Beatriz showed no such caution; she danced about and shouted for joy, taking me in her arms and kissing me. How can you look so pale, she cried. Our fortunes are made!

We have a long way to go before that is assured, I counseled her. She would hear none of it, though, and I worried that she would doom the whole enterprise with her injudiciousness. I sealed up the chest and put it back in its hiding place, ignoring her pleas that I should give her a coin or two right then just to look at. Then I carefully replaced the stones, working at it for some hours to ensure that nothing looked out of place. I left her, saying that I would return in the morning and that then we would flee the city, so she should ready herself for a journey. Until then she was not to disturb the treasure, which caused her to pout for a moment, but her excitement at the adventure we were about to embark on soon overwhelmed that.

I will await you with all my heart, she said to me as I left, and I believed it, fool that I was.

When I arrived the next morning, with all my worldly possessions upon my person, she seized me in a passionate embrace. Such was the frenzy of her ecstasy that I could not dissuade her and, though I feared what should happen if we tarried, I relented and we went to her bedchamber to practice those intimacies of which you are unfamiliar. It was in the midst of this, as she urged me on, that I heard a man cursing me and Our Lord. I did not need to look to know that it was Don Tadeo, who had for some reason come calling on his mistress that morning. It did not seem an opportune time to question him on the fact as he drew his sword and swore to exact vengeance upon me, while Doña Beatriz cried out.

Oh, thank goodness you're here, Tadeo, she said. I just couldn't stop him.

I will deal with you later, my master said to her.

I decided not to tarry a moment longer and seized what clothes of mine I could and threw myself out the window, knocking myself senseless on the shutters as I went. I ended up sprawled in the alley, covered in filth. I could hear Don Tadeo's cries of rage as he made his way down from Doña Beatriz' quarters, and quickly regained myself, putting on my breeches and shirt as I went. I was barefooted, having left my boots in Doña Beatriz' bedchamber. Even then I still was fool enough to believe I would collect them again.

My plan, decided on in a moment as I ran down the street, was to go to my friend Don Antonio's, for I felt certain that Don Tadeo would go to my quarters, expecting that I would return there eventually. I could then return to Doña Beatriz and the treasure and we could make our escape.

The first part went off without a hitch; I found Don Antonio at home and beseeched him to take me in, giving him some tale or other to explain my difficulties. He went out to buy me some clothes and boots, and when he returned we left for Doña Beatriz', where I had promised to repay him for his trouble. We never made it, for whom should we encounter when we came around the corner but Don Tadeo, along with Don Lope and the Alcalde. We had our swords drawn in an instant and the street filled with shouting: Don Antonio and the Alcalde crying out for calm, Don Tadeo calling me a thief, Don Lope shouting that I was a murderer and worse, while I cursed them all for dogs.

At last the din quieted and we began to circle each other warily, our swords waving in the air. My only thought was for Doña Beatriz and the treasure lying in her hearth. I was willing to do whatever was necessary to allow me to reach that goal, even if it meant running through the three men who opposed me.

Don Tadeo was spoiling for a fight, his blood still hot from seeing me in the arms of his mistress. I see you have found some boots, he said to me.

I see you are wearing mine, I replied, and we fell to blows.

Don Antonio was poor with the sword and he was quickly run through. Don Tadeo followed him, my blade piercing his heart. Don Lope and the Alcalde overwhelmed me, landing several telling blows. I surrendered to their mercy at last and the Alcalde seized me by the belt and began to drag me to the jail. As we went, Don Lope promised me that I would pay at last for what I had done to his friends. I knew he was right, for I had no chance of a fair trial and no influential friends left in Cuzco, with both Don Tadeo and Don Antonio dead on the street. And here I was, the cause of it.

I knew that my very life might be at stake and so, chancing it all, I surreptitiously loosened the belt that the Alcalde held me by and waited for my chance. It came as we entered the next street. As we passed by a church I slipped free of the Alcalde's grasp, leaving him only a belt and no man, and ran to the church, passing into that sanctuary before either man had a chance to react.

Oh cruel existence, I deserve all the ill that has befallen me. You have told me so many times and in this, I must admit, you are right. My great friend Don Tadeo, my master, who had never failed to show me kindness, to help me when I was in need, was dead by my hand over a woman and some silver. The shame of this has never left my spirit. Because Our Lord is just, I was forced to witness Don Tadeo's funeral from the rafters of the church where I had taken sanctuary. Oh the misery I felt, both for my master and Don Antonio gone to their reward, and for myself and all I had squandered.

My own situation was still very precarious, for though I had been granted refuge in the church, the Alcalde and Don Lope had set sentries to watch all the exits day and night. It was a state of siege I found myself in, and I knew they would not relent. Although they allowed all and sundry to enter the church, they managed to stop any of my remaining friends. It seemed they knew everyone I was on good terms with, which was an impressive and terrifying feat. Only the holy priests within offered me any aid, giving me a bed to sleep on in their quarters and sharing their food with me.

I passed my days giving confession, recounting the sorrowful events that had led to my entrapment there, and the false vendetta that had been sworn against me by the powerful in that fair city. I took mass daily as well, and lived as piously as I had while in the cloister. A strange irony, no doubt, that I should have come to that impasse after all I had done to escape the chains of that earlier life. My closest companion those long days, though the holy priests showed me nothing but kindness, was a young Indian boy named Diego Poblete, a ladino, who served there as a sacristán. They were teaching him his letters and I helped him with it, as his dream was to become a holy monk of the Franciscans.

When I had gained the boy's confidence I asked him to take a message to my friend Don Mariano, who ran a gaming house I had often frequented. This he did gladly for me, running back and forth, carrying messages between the two of us, so that I was informed of what was happening beyond the church. It was all poor news. The Alcalde had issued a decree promising a reward for my capture and had warned all in Cuzco against offering me any aid. Meanwhile, the guard he had set kept its unceasing watch, offering me no opportunity to slip away.

The other news Don Mariano had for me concerned Doña Beatriz. It seemed she had disappeared, presumably fleeing Cuzco the day I had killed Don Tadeo. The story from her friends was that she had feared retribution from the Alcalde or some other of Don Tadeo's allies for cuckolding him. I, of course, knew the truth of the thing: she had seized her chance and gone off with all the silver. In fact, the more I considered the matter, I realized that this had almost certainly been her plan all along. How else had Don Tadeo happened upon us that morning? It was not mere chance— she had invited him, knowing I would be there, and had aroused my passion so that there could be no doubt as to the nature of our association. With the two of us occupied in our feud she had all the time in the world to make her escape.

I had thought her a devious and petty woman, given to whining, and she had played the part better than I had played mine. I never once suspected what she was about. Now that I knew the truth, my ardor for her was redoubled. What a marvelous woman! Such cunning and intelligence to play us all for fools. Had I known, I would have sworn my devotion to her, asking for nothing in return. It was not to be, but I grieved for the lost chance as I grieved for my dead friends.

Knowing then that I was well and truly on my own, I began to take up a vigil in various parts of the church where I could watch the guard throughout the day and into the night. I searched for any sign of weakness, perhaps some men, bored and given to drink or cards, but found none that I could exploit. I was trapped, and the Alcalde showed no sign of relenting in his siege, even as it entered its third week. I was grasping for any piece of hope I could muster, but was offered only misery. Those days were dark indeed.

And they only became darker. I was at my vigil one evening near one of the confessionals, where I had a plain view of the main doors of the church, which the holy priests kept open through the night at the request of the Alcalde. Normally I would have been elsewhere, hidden from the sight of those on the street, but that day I was feeling bold. As I was idling, enjoying the glares of those who wanted only to seize me, I saw him in the shadows just beyond the glare of the torches of the guard. It was his eyes I noticed first, the blue piercing the night. He stepped forward into the torchlight, his gaze locking on to mine, and I could see on his neck the grotesque scar where I had wounded him. I tried to summon a smile at the sight of that, but my courage failed me and I had to look away in fright.

The Stranger stayed watch the whole night, as did I in turn. He was still there in the morning when I went to mass, and again in the evening as I prepared for bed, and the next day too, always standing just beyond the circle of light of those on guard, his fierce eyes seeming to summon me forth. I did not, though a part of me longed to. I wanted only to be done with this mad siege, which seemed then to have my doom as its only possible conclusion. I resisted, though, for I knew that end would come soon enough, one way or another, and then I truly knew despair.

CITY OF THE VANISHED

HOW I SHIVER to think of those long days and nights that I spent under the vengeful gaze of Don Lope and the Stranger in the Church of San Sebastián. That such a quiet and humble church, in so peaceful a district of Cuzco, should be the scene of such terrible events is surely a sign of the utter corruption of all things in this world. Such thoughts were heavy on my mind then, for the Stranger had managed to invade my dreams, even as he haunted my waking hours, which we spent locked in a strange sort of dance. My nightmares of him in endless pursuit of me would drive me from the quarters I had been given to wander the candlelit nave, only to find him watching me from the darkness of the street. Throughout it all, he acted as though he had all the time in creation to await my emergence from those sacred confines into his profane and bloody embrace. Perhaps he did.

My present thoughts do not lie in those days, they are ever focused on my current circumstance, little changed from where I found myself then. It leaves a bitter taste in my mouth. I have made my complaints plain about the burdens you have placed on me, in addition to the other crueler punishments you have meted out, about which I will not speak now. It matters not; you persist in your persecution of me, demanding that I answer for crimes that I have not committed. You refuse to believe a word I speak and punish me for the lies you say I have written in this document. Yet I swear upon all that is holy that every word is true.

It matters little what I say; you will not hear it. But I know who does have your ear in these matters, and his lies will be exposed soon enough, I promise you. That is why I persist in this task, though I consider it a fool's errand, intended only to incriminate me further in your eyes, regardless of what I should write or say. I know that my patience and virtue shall be rewarded in the end, as is just and righteous. I look toward that day with a serene and clear conscience, while yours I know is stained.

I am saddened that we have come to this terrible impasse, for I placed my entire trust in you from the very beginning of this sordid affair. Each time I have offered forth my hand in friendship you pushed it aside, preferring to come at me with a dagger's cutting edge. I say again, though you will not believe me, that I am only trying to help. You do not understand the danger you are in, though soon enough you will. Perhaps then you will realize who your true friends are.

I fear it will be too late, though. You will have to find your forgiveness in heaven for what you have done to me. Let me only say now and be done: you seek a tyranny over my very soul and you shall not have it!

My salvation in San Sebastián was the young ladino boy Diego. I owe him my life, I know—a debt, sadly, I did not repay. He kept the madness that was slowly poisoning my being from spreading. It was to he that I always turned those days when, no matter whether my eyes were open or closed, I saw the Stranger and I fell to trembling. To distract me from my miserable state he would ask me to recount the many adventures I had undertaken, for he thought, no doubt because of all the attention I was receiving from such important personages as the Alcalde and the treasurer of the city, that I must be someone of great renown.

I did nothing to dissuade him from this false impression, telling him grand tales of the triumphs I had achieved, the failures I had endured and the numerous impossible situations I had managed to extricate myself from. How he reconciled the image I crafted for him with the pathetic individual before him, who often fell to weeping without cause and seemed frightened by the merest shifting of the afternoon shadows, I do not know. If I had half the powers I granted myself I should have been able to magic myself from the church without anyone being the wiser.

In truth, I suspect he knew what I said was mostly bluster, for he was not so simple as that. We were not so far apart in age, and I had given myself enough adventures to last several lifetimes. He enjoyed my company, though, and I think he knew the comfort such tales provided me in those empty hours when I had only my own worry to feast upon my reason. Yes, Diego was as kind a man as I have known, though he was but an Indian. The fathers of the church would say that it was proof that all Indians can be good subjects of the Crown, and perhaps they are right.

Certainly Diego was a fine example. He had been born in the village of Calca near Cuzco, his parents important members of the community. His mother died giving birth to his sister a year later and his father remarried. When he was five his father died of the pox, an affliction for which the natives seem to have an especial weakness for. It is a terrible ailment; I myself have the scars on my cheeks from my battle with the scourge. Diego had an elder brother, Julio, who became the patriarch of the family and was married to his father's wife, a girl named Catalina.

All seemed well, but the Cacique of that village was a brutal, jealous man. He became enamored with Catalina, demanding that she be given over to him. When Julio refused, for the girl was pregnant with his child, the Cacique conspired with the local Corregidor to place some false charges against him. Witnesses were found to say that Julio had done such and such a thing, and he was sentenced to ten years' hard labor among the savages of Chile. The family's meager property was seized by the Corregidor, and the Cacique forced Catalina to become his consort.

Diego and his younger sister found themselves without a home and, with no means to support themselves, they were reduced to a life of beggary. They were chased from the village by the Corregidor and found their way to Cuzco, where they passed many hard months living by their wits. They had such a difficult time of it that Diego was forced to give away his sister, Guadalupe, to a mestizo, who said that a girl was needed in his master's house to work in the kitchen. So dire was their situation that Diego could only hope what he said was true. It may well have been, though I imagine the girl was little better than a slave.

Diego had continued his life on the streets for some years until a Pedro de Cardenado, the parish priest at San Sebastián, had befriended him and given him some tasks in exchange for a bit of food. He had quickly taken note of the boy's intelligence and had brought Diego to God and begun to teach him of his works. So began Diego's life at San Sebastián and from these humble beginnings he had risen to become sacristan.

I too recognized the boy's cleverness, and used him as a messenger to those I knew and could trust so that I might know what was happening beyond the walls of the church. None of what he told me offered any hope. I had thought, foolishly it seemed, that the Alcalde's resolve would wither as a flower in autumn, the demands of his office calling his attention elsewhere as the days and weeks slowly ticked by. The reality was quite the opposite, for however much he had begun his proceedings out of obligation to his friendship with Don Lope, the more obstinate I was in my refusal to submit myself to his justice, the greater his desire to see that I faced it.

The watch set upon San Sebastián did not decline as the days and weeks ticked by, the hours becoming endless and hope seeping from my soul; instead the Alcalde and Don Lope found more and more men to stand sentry against me. The coin it must have cost them I cannot imagine. And each night the Stranger was there in the darkness, waiting. Diego proved extremely useful, for he could pass by this guard without rousing suspicion. In fact, with so many of the same men about every morning and afternoon, he soon befriended several of the guards and passed on what they told him.

I stored whatever morsels of information he was able to provide and kept my own vigil. I watched my watchers, noting their patterns each day, and tried to discern the chink in their armor that would be my salvation. This task and the boy's companionship kept my melancholy at bay, though that storm continually threatened the horizon.

At last the sight of the Stranger watching me from the shadows, his eyes telling me that my dreams of the horrors he would visit upon my person would in time become all too real, was too much. I had to escape San Sebastián and Cuzco and fly as far away as possible, so I set about crafting a plan. Normally I would have used the night to shelter my escape, but the aid it offered me was negated entirely by the presence of the Stranger and his terrible powers. That he had managed to survive our earlier confrontation told me that he was not a man in any sense that you or I would use, but rather a devil incarnate with all the magick that a demon might have upon this earth. I could not hope to defeat him, and certainly I could not evade him along with all the others who maintained the siege. Instead I determined to flee during the day, though it offered me little protection. But the Stranger was not present among the watchers, as near as I could tell, during the daylight hours so, by necessity, it offered my best chance. But how to slip by the guard without attracting notice when I did not have darkness and obscurity as my ally?

I turned instead to my allies of blood and flesh within Cuzco, those friends whom I knew I could trust and would not turn from me, no matter the threats and blandishments Don Lope and the Alcalde might offer. Here Diego was invaluable, for I sent him to my friend Don Mariano and a few others to ask for their aid and to explain what I had in mind. They in turn brought word to others they trusted and, when all was prepared, sent word through Diego to that effect. Here I acted quickly, for I suspected that Don Lope had his men following Diego and I needed to set things in motion before they realized what was afoot.

I chose the following Sunday, for the church would be at its busiest that day and the crowd would offer me greater cover. Don Mariano had sent me a new suit through Diego, which I wore in the hopes of providing a moment's distraction from the watch, who had no doubt grown used to the usual frock that I had been forced to wear for the two months I had been under their gaze. As the church filled with parishioners and mass began, I hid myself amongst them, my hat pulled low. I spied a few of Don Lope's men among the worshipers and saw, to my delight, that they were scanning those gathered for a sign of me, knowing that I normally took mass at this time.

At the conclusion of mass the crowd began to let out into the street where the watch was kept, and I put my plan into action. Don Mariano had engaged two harlots to create a disturbance to draw the attention of the crowd. One of them, a lovely morenasa named Teresa, had spent the morning on the streets around the church selling candies, while the other, a mestiza named Geronima, arranged to pass by Teresa as she was selling her wares to those let out from the service. Teresa feigned to noticing Geronima in turn and immediately confronted her, calling her a whore and all manner of things. Geronima responded in kind, and they fell upon each other, scratching at each other's faces and pulling their hair, creating a tremendous racket.

This had the desired effect, for the crowd exiting the church was drawn toward spectacle. The result was that the street was filled with a milling group of people, trying to make room for the two combatants, mingling with those keeping watch against me. The guards could not resist turning to see what was happening as well, for most of them were now two months into the siege and had long since grown bored with their uneventful duty. In the midst of the crowd, having attended mass, was one Pablo Vallojil, an Indian from Guamanga, and a servant of Don Mariano's. He was the ostensible cause of the battle between the two women, and when he had announced his presence to the assembled they both turned and set upon him as one.

Pablo drew his sword, saying that he would see an end to them both for so dishonoring him before the home of Our Lord. There was great deal of nonsense said back and forth between he and the ladies, with members of the crowd joining in and choosing their side of the dispute. Pablo declared he would suffer these harlots' insults no more and took after them, brandishing his sword. They both fled toward the Alcalde's watch, and those honorable men responded by raising their swords against Pablo. A flurry of threats were uttered back and forth as Pablo demanded to be given the satisfaction of punishing these recalcitrant women, while the Alcalde's men dismissed him as an Indian who had passed beyond all reason and sense.

It was then that Don Mariano and two of his friends happened upon the scene and came to Pablo's aid, demanding the arrest of Teresa and Geronima. The Alcalde's men refused, saying that by rights Pablo and Don Mariano should be arrested. Further insults were traded and soon everyone's swords were drawn and a melee resulted that sent the still-gathered crowd into a seething turmoil, as those nearest to the fight tried to get clear of the blades, while those at the back tried to get nearer to better see what was taking place.

I was in the midst of all this, having exited the church with the crowd at the end of mass. As the incidents had developed I had stayed toward the back of the gathering, nearer the church, but when the fight between the guards and Don Mariano broke out I seized my chance and began to slip through the crowd, hoping, of course, to make a break while the Alcalde's men were otherwise preoccupied. I kept my head low and had my cloak drawn up high over my shoulders, so that between it and my hat little of face was shown. Moving at an angle away from the fight, but staying within the assemblage, I went, neither slowly nor quickly, being careful not to meet anyone's gaze, until the crowd began to dissipate and I could see the open streets before me. Though every fiber of my being demanded that I flee then and there, I kept my wits and walked steadily on, a man about his business..

Just as I thought myself free, a hand seized my shoulder and spun me about, nearly yanking my arm free from my torso, and I found myself face to face with Don Lope himself. I gave a shout and he snarled at me: You are the devil himself.

Better that than his sentinel and pander, was my reply.

I'll see that your corpse is befouled for what you have done to my friends, he said.

Your friend with the blue eyes knows a great deal about fouling corpses, I said to him with an insolent grin. He shall be a great help to you.

Before he could reply I slipped a dagger from within my cloak and lunged at him. He tried to leap out of my way, reaching for his rapier as he did so, but the crowd still pressed about us and he was unable to elude my dagger, which caught him flush in the thigh. I had been trying for his guts, but I did not dare tarry to see the job done. Our commotion had drawn the attention of those nearby, including some of the Alcalde's men, who shouted at their companions still occupied with Don Mariano and Pablo. They abandoned their cause and began to push their way through the crowd for me.

A maelstrom of people engulfed me, people running every which way, unsure who exactly the combatants of this new struggle were and terrified of being inadvertently caught in it. I pulled my dagger free of Don Lope's leg and spat on him before fleeing, darting in and out of the mob of people, heading toward the far end of the street, which still appeared blessedly wide and empty. Behind me I could hear the cries of the Alcalde's men letting their fellows know where I was in the crowd. I tried ducking down so that I would be harder to spy, but I think it did me little good.

Again, just as before, I reached the crowd's edge, even farther from the church now, and had the briefest surge of hope at the freedom that awaited me in but a few brief steps. But, as before, I was thwarted. The Alcalde appeared at the end of the street at the head of a force of a dozen men, all advancing with swords drawn. He spotted me immediately and, pointing at me with his sword, shouted to his men that there would be twenty reales for the one who could run me through. The fiends set off at a run, sending the crowd into even greater torment.

Seeing this, I abandoned my attempt to escape and tried to return to the church. The Alcalde's men seemed to be everywhere in the crowd, swords raised and snarling at people to get out of the way. I could not see Don Mariano and Pablo, and I feared the worst. Still, I could not think of them at the moment, not when my own life lay in the balance. I tried again to wend my way through the crowd, ducking low and hoping to escape notice, but I quickly realized it was no use with the Alcalde's men bearing down on me.

Knowing they would soon have me surrounded, I took off at a run, throwing aside anyone who happened to be in my way. The Alcalde's men came at me from all sides, swinging and lunging with their swords, but I managed to escape them with only a few glancing blows catching me. Bruised and bleeding, I sprinted up the stairs to the church's entrance, my pursuers only a step or two behind. I threw myself across the threshold before they could seize me and fell at the feet of Father Pedro, begging him for salvation and mercy. Outside I could hear the Alcalde snarl in anguish.

After my failed escape I took to bed, ostensibly because of the wounds I had suffered at the hands of the Alcalde's men. In truth, they were minor and healed easily. My troubles lay within my soul, for I despaired of ever being free of that place. It seemed I would have to face the Stranger if I should hope to escape, and I knew as well that I had no hope of besting him. I was doomed to this half-life, stalked by the devil and his minions every step of every day. Oh, it is no wonder that I was lost to tears and misery for days, my thoughts so black I had energy only to sleep.

It is hard to write of those terrible days, to think again of my thoughts, so black that I even gave credence to that which Our Lord forbids, self-murder. I stayed my hand then, but only just. It is harder still, of course, because my current predicament so mirrors that of this earlier imprisonment. No good can come of the days to follow; this I know more than you can ever understand. I have tried to tell you, but you have not listened. Perhaps in reading this you will realize what I speak of, but I do not think it possible. You are too convinced, too strident in your beliefs and narrow understanding of this world to be able to see the danger you have placed yourself in. I will be punished for my sins and crimes, and that is all that you concern yourself with, never mind that a greater evil is being perpetrated in your name.

But enough! I shall not let my bitterness infect my tale, and your part in it still awaits to be told.

Don Mariano and Pablo had managed to survive their encounter with the Alcalde's men and had escaped without arrest, as had the two harlots. In their pursuit of me the Alcalde's men had apparently forgotten all others. Diego brought me this news while I lay in bed, and it did hearten me. Worse tidings soon followed, though, for when I sent Diego back to give my thanks to Don Mariano for what he had done, the boy found him hanging from the doorway of his establishment, the blood drained from his face and a strange rune marked upon his forehead.

Diego's face was pale as a ghost when he told me of what he had seen, and I knew the terror that he felt, for there could only be one hand behind that desecration and I had felt his dagger at my throat before. Hearing this news plunged me even deeper into despair, and I was unable to eat for some days. Diego nursed me as though I were an invalid awaiting only the embrace of Our Lord, and in a way I was, for I could see no other alternative that would free me from my predicament.

When I had at last shaken free of the black humor that infected my senses, Father Cardenado was awaiting me with a proposal. During my convalescence he had taken it upon himself to speak with the Alcalde, praising me as a kind and generous soul who had done much to help the church during my time their. He offered, if the Alcalde was so inclined, to arrange for a meeting between we two enemies, in his presence and under a flag of truce, to see if there were some way beyond our impasse. The Alcalde, according to Father Cardenado, had been most eager to take him up on his offer, and so I was reluctantly forced to agree, though I held out little hope of anything coming of this parley.

We met in the sacristy. The two of us sat uneasily across from each other, as though we each expected the other to spring up at a moment's notice and strike, destroying the sanctity of that holy place. Father Cardenado smiled and thanked us both for joining him, and then asked what might be done to settle things to the satisfaction of all involved.

He must stand trial, the Alcalde said to the Father, refusing to address me directly. Don Lope, as honorable a man as can be found in this fair city, I fear will lose his leg. And this man is the cause. To say nothing of the crimes that brought him to your sanctuary in the first place.

Father Cardenado nodded and turned to me. I replied, looking at him as well, that I had no fear of a trial, provided it was fair and I had the opportunity to speak and defend myself.

Then why does he remain here and scheme to escape without facing his accusers as is just, the Alcalde demanded.

I do not fear that opportunity. I embrace it, I told them both. It is just that I cannot believe that I, in truth, will be given the chance.

Lies, the Alcalde cried.

What do you mean, Father Cardenado asked me, ignoring the other man. A braver man than Pedro de Cardenado I have not encountered, to stand up to the Alcalde of the city without so much as batting an eyelash.

I told them of what had happened to my friend Don Mariano and of my earlier encounter with Don Lope and the Stranger, which had started the entire ordeal. It is my fear, I said to them, that those two men will not allow me to reach a trial or to survive whatever punishment the Alcalde deems just. They wish only my blood.

This sent the Alcalde into a fury. He called me a liar and a charlatan, the wearer of a thousand masks. His words stirred my ire, but good sense prevented me from responding to him in kind.

That this false man, the Alcalde said, should impugn my office, suggest that the proceedings I lead would be unfair and that Don Lope, one of the great men of this city, should be the one to subvert them is beyond belief.

Father Cardenado tried to calm the Alcalde, saying that I had obviously meant no disrespect by my words. I was little more than a youth after all and, naturally, feared being taken advantage of by those in positions of authority. I did nothing to help my cause, sadly, for I was unable to resist a jibe directed at the Alcalde, saying that unless I was certain that he was not a servant of the devil himself I could not chance putting my soul at his mercy. That was all the Alcalde could bear. He stood up and told the Father that he was a servant of the Crown and that if he, Father Cardenado, wished to be in league with a blasphemer such as me then that was his choice, but he should not be surprised if the Inquisition became involved.

With that he left and Father Cardenado sighed and looked at me very sadly, and would say no more to me. I felt very sorry for what I had done. It had not been my intention to enseam a man so noble of intention as the Father in my affairs, yet I had been unable to resist baiting the Alcalde. I have always been so, given to fits of anger and pique, forever willing to twist the dagger deeper and speak with a barbed tongue, though the blade should be turned back on me. Even now my anger stirs me to say hateful things to you, though we have on occasion been friends, and though my fate now rests in your hands.

Can one change one's nature, or are we condemned to our errors, forever having to beg forgiveness of those we have wronged?

In the weeks that followed my confrontation with the Alcalde, the guard outside the church doubled in size, with more than a dozen men keeping watch both night and day. The Alcalde himself often came during the day to see that his orders were being carried out and, of course, the Stranger kept up his nightly vigil. I could not bear to face his gaze anymore, for my deeds had told him I knew I was no match for him, and it seemed to only grant him further power.

My only satisfaction at this development was the vain hope that both the Alcalde and Don Lope were bankrupting themselves keeping up this siege. Men such as that never seem to want for coin, always having a dozen or a hundred men who are in their debt and whom they can hold to account. It was for this reason I knew that I would never be safe in the Viceroyalty, even if I somehow managed to escape the confines of San Sebastián. Even here, under the protection of Father Cardenado, I could not be certain of being safe. Though I trusted Don Lope and the Alcalde not to bloody the sanctity of Our Lord, I had no doubt that the Stranger would, if the opportunity presented itself.

I had to escape, then, but how? I was at my wits' end; the siege had crippled my soul and, after the debacle of my last escape attempt, and the murder of Don Mariano that had resulted from it, I was no longer sure of my own mind. It was as though I were afflicted by some strange disease that caused tremors in my hands and spirit, made my thoughts turn morose and angry at an instant and sent me to bed for no reason beyond an unshakeable despair. The days and weeks passed and my strange melancholy persisted until I think Father Cardenado and Diego worried that I would become an invalid, weak in body and soul.

It was Diego who spared me from my own dark thoughts and helped me to return to me my strength. He would often come to pass the hours as I lay in bed in a pitiful state. I believe Father Cardenado had requested that he do so, for the priest feared that I would commit some unholy act if I were left alone. The boy tried to distract me with tales of his life and stories that he had heard on the street. He had befriended several of the guard who kept watch on me, and they had taken to bragging to him of their prowess with women and the sword, and these tales he repeated to me for my amusement.

After a time he grew even bolder and confessed to me that he had no interest in the life of a monk as he had led Father Cardenado and the others believe. He was only staying with them out of a sense of obligation to the kindness they had shown him. I asked him where he would go and what he would do if he were to leave. Here he grew pensive and his face darkened with emotion, as though an internal struggle were underway. One side emerged victorious and he said to me: I would return to my people.

Do the Corregidor and Cacique not still hold sway in your village, I said to him. They would react very poorly if you returned.

That was not his intention, he explained, for his village was still not safe for him. It seemed that Julio had escaped the presidio where he had been sent and, rather than returning to his village or Cuzco, where he was certain to be arrested, he had fled deep into the Andes. There he had come across what he described as the last redoubt of the once mighty Incan Empire. He had managed to send word to Diego, apparently Father Cardenado had managed to inform Julio of Diego's whereabouts and situation while he was imprisoned.

I told Diego frankly that I doubted his brother's words, for the last Incan stronghold had been captured some thirty years before and Tupac Amaru, the last emperor, had been executed. By all accounts the city of Vilcabamba had been destroyed and now lay abandoned, the region and its natives now under the rule of the Crown. There had been no word of any who had escaped, nor had there been any claimants to that dead throne. I feared he was being led astray—to what ends I could not say, but he insisted that his brother would do no such thing, that the place existed.

It was abandoned and lost, you see, he explained to me, but then, when your kind came to these lands some of our people fled and discovered it and made it their home.

My face must have told him how I felt about what he said, for he continued on without heed. You could help me reach it. I do not think I could make the journey alone and I am sure you would be given a great reward for your help.

The lost city, according to him, was as great and marvelous as Cuzco had been upon Pizarro's arrival, with vast temples to their heathen gods. There was, according to Diego, treasure of unimaginable proportions contained in those temples, and his brother was certain that there were sources of gold and silver nearby. From everything that he said it seemed to be the fabled El Dorado. I knew that most of this was said for my benefit, to play on my native greed. Did he think me as mad as Aguirre?

Not likely, but, the question was, to what end was Diego plying me with such blandishments? Perhaps he did truly wish to seek out his brother and live amongst his people, in which case I knew that I should dissuade him, for his life here was one in service to Our Lord. Were he to leave, to live amongst the heathens, he would assure his soul's eternal damnation. The other possibility, which gave me some pause, was that the entire tale was a lie intended to draw me from my sanctuary and into the arms of the Alcalde.

The Indians do have treacherous hearts, which they cover with a mask of demure obedience, as I'm sure you know. How many have claimed Our Lord as their savior only to return to the barbaric practices of their fallen gods? It should not have surprised me that Diego might have many faces, and yet it did, for he seemed such an innocent, untouched by the meaner things in life. His own past put that to lie, of course, but it was hard in our conversations not to see in him an unblemished creature, as Adam was before Eve was tempted by the serpent.

In the days that followed he returned again and again to the tale of his brother and the lost city of gold, each time providing me further details on its whereabouts, as though to prove the truth of his other words. He would lament that he could not undertake the journey to this fabled place, for it was too arduous for a boy to manage on his own. The reward that I would be due to receive also continued to grow. One day, after he had begun his sorry tale again, I asked him, keeping my face a picture of innocence, why he was confiding this precious information in me.

You are my friend, he said to me in earnest, and I cannot undertake such an adventure on my own.

I smiled at him. And I am such a person to help you, you think?

Oh yes, he said eagerly. With all that you have done, I would feel safe in your hands.

And you trust me, I asked him.

With my life, he said immediately. You have shown me great kindness since you came. I tried to repay it by helping you escape. I will gladly assist you again. Then you can aid me on my journey and I am sure that Julio and his people will be able to grant you a fine reward.

I was quite certain that they would not, but I agreed with him that it seemed a fair deal. The problem, as I said to him, was still how to escape the clutches of the Alcalde.

He agreed that this seemed an insurmountable task, but he was certain there was a way. Had I not escaped from more difficult situations in the past? If the stories I had told him had an ounce of truth that would have been so, but of course I had embroidered and embellished to such a degree that I could no longer recall even a half of what I had said to him. I mentioned none of this, telling him instead that, though this situation might not appear as dire as some of the others, it was in fact the most precarious I had been in, for reasons he could not begin to understand. There were great powers at work here, I intimated, and would say no more.

This seemed to satisfy him, at least for the moment, though he said again that he believed in me, that I would think of a means of escape. Though I knew his confidence was falsely placed it still heartened me, and after he had left me to my thoughts I found myself pondering again how I might thwart the Stranger and his foul desires. I would not let this moment be the end, I decided, not when I had but tasted glorious freedom so briefly. I had not begun to drink my fill.

Your women have been to see me and they will verify that my claims are true. How often must they inspect me before you will take me at my word? I suspect it is your guilt at what you have done to me that drives you to seek some other explanation for what has happened. Perhaps when I have written all this it will convince you, but I think not. Nothing has, not since I took you at your word and put my trust in you, a trust you have broken time and time again. How heavy my heart is to think of it.

The solution to my insoluble problem at San Sebastián was, if I may say so, ingenious. You will probably see more evidence of my deviousness. Was I supposed to meekly submit myself to the depredations of Don Lope and the Stranger? For you that would be the proper and honorable course of action, but that way lay death and worse, so I refused it. Instead, I set myself upon another path.

The spark of the idea that would set me free came one afternoon as I idled in the nave adjacent to the main doors of the church. The guard had not noticed my presence, for in my months of imprisonment I had become very skilled at moving about while escaping their notice, even while I was standing right before them. Only the Stranger was able to spy me with ease, even on the darkest of nights. My last attempted flight had, unfortunately, apprised the Alcalde and Don Lope as to my skills and, as a result, they had begun to stop each man who came out of the church. They were especially attentive after mass, causing a crowd to bottleneck at the entrances as they made each man take off his hat and show his face to them.

I was watching the men on duty carry out their routine with two Andalusians, who had called on Father Cardenado that day, when I saw something that gave me pause. A castiza woman, who had come to pay her devotions and light a candle to Our Lady of Mercy, left at nearly the same moment as the Andalusian gentlemen, and she was given a cursory glance before the guard let her pass. There, I realized, was my opportunity, for who could more easily pass as a woman than I? Even if the guard should recognize me somehow and arrest me, they could not very well claim that I was the man they sought, for any inspection that they carried out would show otherwise.

I kept this thought to myself, biding my time and letting my hair grow out. I pretended that I was still as morose and melancholy as

I had been earlier, spending days in bed and talking to Diego as though my time was near its end. He kept at his attempts to draw me out, telling me ever-greater tales of the lost city and the blandishments I was certain to receive if I should aid him. His persistence in the matter only served to further convince me that he was in league with the Alcalde, for it was not in his character to act so.

I allowed myself, slowly, over a period of weeks, to appear to be seduced by his lies. When I had at last swore to him that I would assist him in his journey should he help me escape, he presented to me a plan to get past the Alcalde's blockade. This plan, he swore upon his eternal soul, had come to him while he was leaving the church to run some errands for Father Cardenado. The guards, he noted, hardly paid him any mind when he passed by, so he could easily create some sort of distraction among them that I could use to escape.

You spend quite a lot of your days talking with those fellows, I said to him.

Yes, he said, quite oblivious to my meaning. They are always bored and ready to talk and play jokes on me. That is why they will never suspect me of anything.

I seized him by the shoulders then and he cried out in pain as I demanded to know whether he was in league with them. He swore again and again that he was not, even as I told him that he was too great a fool to come up with any plan that could trick these men, that it had to be they who had come to him with the idea. He was but the implement they had selected. This made him angry, and he cursed me, saying that I was the fool and that he was only trying to help, for I had proven myself to be a great friend. If I did not want his help I could find my own way out from my predicament. I pretended to be mollified and asked him what he proposed.

He dug into his robe and pulled out a small glass bottle, a little bigger than my fist, and passed it to me. There were Chinese inscriptions painted on the side that I could make no sense of. At a motion from Diego I pulled out the stopper and poured a bit of the contents out into my hand, recognizing immediately that it was filled with some manner of gunpowder.

How did you come by this, I asked him as I returned the powder to the vial.

He shrugged and made a vague motion with one hand as the

other returned the vial to where it was hidden on his person. It is from Manila, he said.

That does not explain how you came to possess it, I said.

He looked at me evasively and then said, shamefaced, I stole it from a merchant.

I nodded as if I accepted this lie as well, and he began to explain his plan. He would, he said, leave the next day to run his morning errands and stop to talk with the guard near the main entrance. As there were always men stationed outside the church, several Indian woman had set up grills upon which they roasted guinea pigs and chicken hearts to sell to the guard. Diego proposed that he would throw this incendiary into one of their fires, causing a fearsome explosion. I was to use the chaos that would follow to flee.

I agreed that this seemed a sensible plan, and together we decided that we would put it in action the following day. My only stipulation, I said, was that I would not venture out if the Stranger was still present, no matter the confusion Diego caused. The boy frowned and looked as though he might argue with me, but my expression told him that I would brook no opposition, so he agreed and together we clasped hands and swore oaths. My hope was that the boy would send word to the Alcalde and that he would ensure that the Stranger stayed away, for I felt certain that the devil would want to be there to witness my capture.

For the rest of the day Diego shared many significant glances with me, so enamored was he with the caper he was a part of. As for me, I played the role as he had written it, and that night I set to work on my own plan, working fiendishly through the darkest hours. Before first light I stole into the cell where Diego slept and laid a hand on his shoulder, startling him at his prayers. He whirled around to face me, a hand raised as if to ward off a blow. I leaned in very close so that our heads nearly touched and he had to meet my eyes.

All is as you have planned it, I asked of him. He nodded, his face gone white.

Good, I said. My life is in your hands, you understand? He nodded again and I gave him a cold smile and squeezed his shoulder, which caused him to wince.

That is well, I said. You shall not see me until we rendezvous tonight. All depends on you. I emphasized that last phrase and he looked at me strangely, as if he did not understand my meaning.

Soon enough he would.

I retreated to my own quarters then, for I had to be quick in what I was about to do. I threw off my clothes and boots and hat and left them on my bed. In their place I put on a dress and shawl of the sort that a Spaniard of a lower station might wear. I had procured these items over the past weeks from one such woman, the wife of a shopkeeper, who came daily to San Sebastián to pray. That had exhausted the last of the coins from the meager stash I had when the Alcalde had arrested me. Now I was well and truly destitute. Reluctantly, I left my clothes and my rapier behind, though it pained me deeply to do so, taking only a dagger that I concealed on my person. Thus I left the markings of one life for those of another and went out into the world.

The church itself was largely empty with everyone at their prayers and ablutions, so I was able to steal my way through unnoticed. After ensuring that the Stranger had absented himself from those in attendance at the watch, I stepped into the street and made my way toward the guard. I passed near them, careful to keep my gaze averted and subservient, as a woman should. As I walked by, the man nearest me looked me over, a small frown crossing his face. I continued on, my pace unchanging, and did not look back, though I could sense the man still watching me as he struggled to think of where he had seen me before. My disguise fooled him, though, all the more because it was not a disguise.

I went on down the street without incident, my step growing lighter as I went. When I came to the first corner I took it, and was out of sight of San Sebastián for the first time in four months. I wanted to cry out for joy, but my excitement proved short-lived, for whom should I see coming down the streets toward me but Don Lope, no doubt hoping to witness my capture. I might have slipped by without his noticing, but the surprise I felt at seeing him perched atop the back of an Indian porter must have been written plain on my face, for he gave me a queer look. Before I had a chance to hurry on and vanish in the bustle of the street, I saw a look of realization pass across his face and he ordered his porter to halt. He demanded that I stop in the same breath and then climbed down from his porter's back and hobbled over to me, wincing and moving slowly on his new wooden leg.

I am at your service, my lord, I said to him, in a demure voice that was not my own.

He looked me over skeptically from head to toe, and with a shake of his own head demanded in a harsh voice: What is your name?

Luisa de Erauso, I said, being careful not to meet his eyes.

No, he said. No, I think not.

He seized me by the arm and dragged me roughly into a nearby alley, motioning for the porter to stand watch at the entrance. I protested meekly that I was an honorable woman and that my husband would see to it that he paid for this injustice. He snorted at my words and pressed me against the wall of the nearest building, grasping at my womanly parts. Not finding what he sought, he started back in surprise.

He was right, Don Lope said, making a warding sign against evil. You are transmutable.

I do not know what you are talking about, my lord, I said, feigning to weep.

Do not take me for a fool, Don Lope said angrily. You are the very figure of the devil, able to take whatever shape you please and put on whatever mask you desire. I do not know how you managed to get past the Alcalde and his men, but I will see that you repay your debt to me. It is a heavy one.

His hand strayed to the sword at his belt. At that moment Diego set off his incendiary outside San Sebastián, and the tremendous noise reached our ears and brought shouts and cries of alarm from those on the street. The startled porter walked away from his post, trying to see what had caused such a ruckus, and even Don Lope turned to look. I seized the moment and sprang at him, the concealed dagger now in my hands. He fumbled for his sword, stumbling backwards on his poor leg, and I was upon him, the dagger at his throat.

This time I will see the job finished, I said to him in my own voice.

He will see that I am avenged, Don Lope said, though his voice trembled as he spoke.

I did not need to ask him who he referred to. Small good it will do you, I said with a laugh, and then I drew my blade across his throat. By the time the porter returned to the alley, I was gone.

You will be horrified, I have no doubt, at my actions, the murder of another, no matter the crimes he was guilty of, no matter that he had been about to act in kind to me. Yet you think nothing of what you do to me, for you have the seal of justice to put to it, and that is enough to put your mind at ease. A criminal heart lurks behind your honorable face. God forgives, but I do not, and you will answer for your crimes soon enough. So do what you can while you are able; the hour grows ever later.

I know little of what occurred in Cuzco in the aftermath of the murder of Don Lope and my escape. I had no doubt I would be blamed for the fiend's death, and that the Stranger would be out on the prowl for me. I needed to leave, the sooner the better, but the problem was where to go. It was a bitter irony that, now that I had engineered my freedom and was able to roam wheresoever I chose, all ports were closed to me. The Alcalde had already sent word to all the local forts and towns that I was to be arrested on sight, and now he would be organizing men to head off in pursuit of me. The trick, then, was to go where they would not suspect me of being. As to that I had some ideas, but first I needed to shed my disguise and get a sword so that I might protect myself.

Having no coin presented certain difficulties, and the last thing I wanted to do, now that I had freed myself from my prison, was to find myself in trouble for theft. Instead I went to the market where I knew Diego went each day and waited, moving about unnoticed by anyone. He came late in the day, my sword under his arm. As he bartered with someone for it, I stole up behind him and clasped him by the shoulder, leaning in to whisper in his ear.

The cut of that blade is familiar, I said to him, putting as much venom into the words as I could summon. He shuddered and his face lost all its color.

You look as if you had seen a dead man, I added, this time loud enough that those around us could hear.

Perhaps I have, he muttered, and started away, leaving the man he was bartering with looking perplexed. I fell in step with the boy and put my arm through his, as though he were my husband escorting me about the city. I pressed him in close, not letting him escape when he tried to shrug me off.

What kind of fool did you take me for, I asked him. Did you think you could betray me and I would not see through your lies?

You thought me fool enough to believe all your lies, he said bitterly to me. I only returned the favor.

I guided him toward a secluded byway where no one was about, and then threw him against the nearest wall, taking my sword from him. You have my clothes and boots as well, I said to him, and he nodded miserably and reached into the pouch at his hip, passing them over.

I had a look at them, making sure all was well, and then looked the boy over. I would give you a beating for what you've done, I told him, but I see the Alcalde has the quicker fists.

He thought I was in league with you, Diego said to me, his voice edged with tears.

I laughed. In a manner of speaking, you were. Did you really expect me to believe that nonsense about your brother?

But it is true, he burst out, unable to contain himself.

I cocked an eye at him and stroked my chin. True, you say. That your brother has escaped to a city of the vanished whose streets are paved with gold? That seems hard to credit.

Diego trembled under my gaze, but his voice when he spoke was firm. My brother did send word to me of the place and begged me to join him. He said it was as a paradise. The Caciques all have much gold and silver, though he did not say from where.

As he said this, an intriguing thought came to me. Who could follow me on a journey to the lost city of a vanished people? The boy and a few other Indians might know of the place, but who would pay any mind to them? Certainly not the Alcalde and the Stranger. And if there should be treasure in the offing, all the better. The more I parsed the idea in my mind, the sounder it seemed. I glanced down at Diego, crouching and miserable at my feet, and saw that his face was marked with a look of fear and revulsion the like I have never seen, as though he had understood my thoughts while I had had them.

Come with me, I said, motioning for him to give me the Indian pouch he wore slung over his shoulder. I stuffed my clothes and boots back in it and then handed him my sword, taking him firmly by the arm again, and set off down the street. Diego tried to flee several times as we went, but each time my strength overwhelmed him. As we grew nearer to the city's edge he began to weep and moan abjectly.

Hush, I said to him. What are these tears? Are you not the one who wanted to go to your brother?

No, he said, I am happy with Father Cardenado. He has been so kind to me.

83

So your thought with that tale was to fatten your purse, I said.

He did not answer me and, as we left Cuzco behind for the mountains and valleys that surrounded her, he entered into a state of near catatonia, unresponsive to any of my entreaties. I was happy for it; I had had enough of his mewling, and it afforded me the opportunity to think about the difficulties that lay before me. I skirted around the villages that neighbored Cuzco, assuming that the Alcalde's word would have reached these places. I stayed in my dress for the same reason, but after we had walked for some hours and darkness had enveloped us I stopped and changed, having no more stomach for hiding.

We walked through most of the night, stopping only for a few hours to allow the boy a bit of rest. He collapsed upon the cold and unforgiving earth and was asleep in an instant. So deep was his slumber that I left him there for a time, feeling no tiredness myself, and stole into a nearby farm to see what food I might gather for us. It was a Spaniard's property, with a great house at its center and a dog on guard. I silenced him easily enough and then slipped into the house and took from the pantry anything that was easy to carry in Diego's pouch.

By the time I had returned, the boy had awoken and wandered off in the darkness. I found him quickly enough, for I was much more at ease in the night than he. Once I had him under my command again we ate a bit of what I had pilfered and then set off, heading toward the coming sun.

I knew the boy had lied to me when he declared himself happy to remain with Father Cardenado at San Sebastián. If that had truly been the case he would not have so willingly betrayed me for the few coins promised him by the Alcalde. What need did he have of those? He was not, I think, given to greed, as so many of us lamentably are. Rather, he was, as I think I have said, more or less an innocent in the world and its ways. The question, then, was why he had lied to me. To what gain? Or was it merely the fact that he was my prisoner that led him to prevaricate and me to suspect him of it? You have not failed to suspect all that I say and all that I have written in this account, yet I have been honest and true with you. Still, I will grant you, with everything else that has happened since our paths have crossed, that your doubt in me is amply justified. I have only myself to blame.

I had the boy set our path and soon we had outstripped all the villages surrounding Cuzco, leaving even the Incan roads behind, and were so high in the mountains that each step required a labored breath. I was soon plagued by the most fearsome of headaches, blinding, like a continuous firing incendiary sparking in my eyes. Diego tried to use my condition to his advantage, for he was apparently unaffected by the dizzying heights we climbed to, fleeing at every opportunity, especially when I was forced to sleep. Bothered as I was by the mountain air, I had no trouble in keeping him near me. No matter how quiet he was, he could not slip past me out of our camps, while I, on the other hand, could come and go as I pleased without him so much as stirring in his slumber.

A greater problem than the altitude began to affect us, for the path we were upon took us away from any populated areas, leaving us to fend for ourselves entirely. We scrounged for food as we went, but the higher up we were the more scarce it became. I hunted a bit, especially at night, but the mountains were barren of game and there was barely enough to sustain us. Soon we were subsisting on herbs and roots and little else.

I knew that Diego was leading me astray, taking me far from the lost city and his brother, hoping that some terrible doom befell me before I realized his subterfuge. That he would share in my fate seemed not to bother him, for the farther we went the more eager he became to lead me on. Perhaps despair had unmoored his reason and he cared not whether he lived or died. For my part, though I knew the boy was laying some trap for me, I made no effort to stop him. I thought it likely I could outlast him in any trial of survival, no matter that the mountains seemed to weaken me more than they did him. Nor did I blame him for his deception—I would have done the same in his case, and no doubt he knew that the arrival of a Spaniard among his brethren could only lead to their doom.

My only care was that he take me far from where the Stranger and the Alcalde were likely to be. I had no doubt that fiend had bent the noble officer of the Crown to his will. Neither man would rest until they had achieved some measure of vengeance against me. This I knew for certain, and it spoiled the pleasure of my regained freedom, as one piece of fruit sends the rest to rot. In a manner of speaking, I had exchanged one prison for another; though I was now free to go where I pleased, I would forever be

85

pursued no matter where I went. My only succor was to disappear. My flight into the mountains with mad Diego breaking the trail was my first such attempt to vanish. Later I would grow skilled in such matters, but those tales remain to be told.

As it was, I was haunted by the pursuit I imagined was at my heels, even in those godforsaken places, so much so that I was happy enough to be led to whatever doom Diego had in store for me. Let us both wallow in misery and terror alone in the mountains, I thought, and if neither of us should ever leave, so be it. Such was the dark tenor of my thoughts, and Diego's many escape attempts did little to improve my company. Most of our journey passed in silence, the boy only speaking when I spoke to him, and, even then, sometimes only under duress, while I was in no mood for conversation.

Our situation seemed only to worsen as each day we went deeper into that mountainous region, even the forests through which we had been moving starting to dissipate, and with them the only thing that had provided us with sustenance. Water became difficult to find as well, for it never rained while we were there and the streams and creeks, which had once been plentiful, became scarce. My thirst and hunger began to work at my mind, leading me to wild flights of imagination. Worst of all was the cold of the region, for we were well into winter by then. Our breath clouded the air and all the water we found was frozen. Both Diego and I shivered through our days, our clothes no match for the elements.

For a time a panther, a rarity in those harsh climes, stalked us, no doubt because we appeared the only feast available to it. As the days went by and I continued to catch sight of the creature— watching us from a ledge above as we passed below along the thin and precipitous trail, or staring with glowing eyes from the darkness as we huddled around the meager fire I had built—I began to suspect it was the Stranger himself who stalked us. I will freely admit I was suffering from a delirium by then, and my fevered thoughts became further inflamed by the idea that the Stranger had somehow transformed himself into that mysterious cat and was now toying with me, prolonging his revenge to make it all the sweeter.

Though I knew I was not of my right mind, I could not shake the conviction from my soul, and I decided I could run no more from those spirits that haunted me. I left the boy one night as he slept in those mountain wastes and began to stalk the beast. I became as an animal upon the earth, attuned to the wind and the intuition of the wilds, tracking the panther as he tracked me. We circled each other on those mountains, each hidden from the other's sight, now in pursuit, now fleeing. For days it seemed this went on, though I had lost all sense of time in my madness, so consumed was I with the confrontation I was certain was about to occur. A duel that I had believed I had escaped had, in fact, merely been postponed.

My memory of that time is hazy, for I neither ate nor slept, but at last I gained the upper hand and managed to steal upon the panther as it crouched in a crevice, no doubt awaiting my appearance to pounce on me. Instead I leapt upon it, dagger in hand, slicing open its throat before it had a chance to react. It let loose a soft growl, more like a moan, and lay beneath me pathetically as its life force drained from it. At that moment I knew that it had not been the Stranger who had pursued me, but a mere beast, and that our confrontation still awaited me. The creature had more cunning than many a man I had chanced to encounter and so, out of respect for my adversary, I drank of its blood and ate its still-warm heart.

The strength this gave me returned me to my senses and I set off in pursuit of the boy, finding him not far from where I had left him, leaning against a tree and nearly insensible. He wept upon seeing me, begging me to leave him to his death. I said I would do no such thing and that our days of playing were at an end. I had let him lead me astray, but now he must set a true path. If he did so, perhaps then I would grant him his wish. He looked at me, an expression bereft of emotion and hope, and without a word set off down the mountain we were upon. Soon we were upon an old road, little used and in poor condition, but of native origin no doubt.

It was two days later, after we had descended into a valley and begun our rise out, that we sighted two men leaning upon a boulder in the distance. Diego took off in a flash, demonstrating far more strength than I had thought remained in him, yelling and screaming for the two men to come to his aid. I followed behind, though more cautiously, trying to give the appearance of being unconcerned. I could see from where I was that the two men were Spaniards by their dress, and I knew that they would be unlikely to believe the boy's pleas over whatever I chose to tell them. Better, I thought, to give them no reason to be suspicious.

Strangely, neither man stirred at our approach, and I saw why as I came near. Diego had already fallen to his knees, wailing in despair and cursing Our Lord for having so forsaken him. Both men were dead, frozen stiff and open-mouthed, as if in laughter. I gathered the boy to me and walked on, he offering no resistance, as I wondered if we had somehow passed beyond this fair realm into some circle of hell from which there was no chance of returning.

The days following our encounter with the dead Spaniards were among the worst I have known. We had no food or water, and the boy became so affected by the lack of these that he continually found himself lost. I believe this was not due to some attempt at deception on his part, for he now knew his only salvation lay in finding his people. His mind had entered some form of deep catatonia, which I knew only food and warmth could cure. I had neither to offer him. The cold was such that we could not even rest for long without risking being unable to awaken from our slumbers.

One morning, as the light crept over the peaks before us and Diego stood looking befuddled at some crossroads or other, I took matters into my hands. I unbuttoned my tunic, exposing my throat and chest to elements, and motioned for Diego to come near. He did so warily and I grasped him firmly, drawing him closer until our lips nearly touched. I drew my dagger, causing him to flinch, but I held him tight and brought the blade to my own throat.

You must drink of this, I said to him, and then I cut myself, not deeply, but enough to draw a steady stream of blood.

He struggled fiercely against me, with all the strength that yet remained in him, but it was not nearly enough to thwart me. I pressed his mouth to my wound, and for a time he was limp against me. The blood wakened his hunger, though, and at last he stirred and began to drink of me. After he had had his fill, I cradled him in my arms and let him sleep, a slumber so deep that I at times wondered if he had passed into the beyond. When he awoke he was restored, the picture of the boy I first met in San Sebastián, his heart all light and innocence. I asked him to take me to his people's lost city and, smiling, he agreed and we set off.

That night, as we cradled each other for warmth, he confessed his reason for trying to lead us both to our deaths. He was, he said, afraid of what would happen should we reach the lost city. Though Julio had asked him to come make a life with him there, Diego feared that his time in San Sebastián had changed him beyond reckoning. He was not the Indian boy his brother had left when he had been exiled and punished—he was a ladino, dressing as a Spaniard did, with our tongue and our mannerisms. He had forgotten much of his people's heathen ways. What, he wondered, would his brother say when he saw this?

His anguish struck a chord with me and still does, for though poor Diego had taken on the dress and customs of the Spaniards, we both knew he would never be seen as one, not truly. And in doing so he had severed himself from what he had been, perhaps for good. For who knew if the path back could be found, time having blown the trail clear. It was a hard thing to face, that he was neither one nor the other now, but he seemed willing to see it through to the end, no matter the outcome.

What I told him, what I tell you now, is the true nature of the world. You will deny it, but those of us like Diego and myself know it for truth. We are all of us transmutable, one thing and another, inhabiting both aspects. Was not Our Lord both Man and God? I will not claim to know enough of your subtle learnings to debate you on the intricacies of this, but it is so. The great Aztecs in Mexico worshiped a god they claimed was both a serpent and a man, so I am told. All of us have these aspects within us, some more than others. If you wish to understand me and all that I have done, this you will have to accept.

We walked for days upon days, at last crossing over the mountains and descending into a vast jungle, the likes of which I had never seen. After the freezing climate of the Andes, the humidity of the jungle was a welcome change. Our way did not become any easier, for there were no trails in the jungle and every footstep required a battle against the vegetation to achieve. Still, we ate well, for the forest provided endless fruits and nuts, to say nothing of the beasts I hunted, and I think we both, Diego and I, felt at ease as we had not since we left San Sebastián.

This, of course, was because our destination loomed before us. Diego would be reunited with his brother and his people, and I would, if what Diego had told me was true, find a fortune beyond all belief. Again I recalled the mad Aguirre and his comrades and their search for El Dorado. They, and so many others, had come to this very jungle, the incomparable Amazon, and had lost their way, but I had someone to guide me. I had, I realized, not allowed myself to truly believe the boy's words until we entered that dense forest from which I could see no escape, but which he navigated with ease.

I had kept such thoughts from my mind, but now they preyed upon me. My dreams were filled with visions of a city filled with natives dressed in gold, worshiping golden idols and eating from golden bowls. Even in my waking moments my mind wandered to such thoughts. The sun itself, when the canopy above opened to allow me a glimpse, seemed afire with molten gold, awaiting the hand of Our Lord to form it. With such thoughts of the riches that awaited me I began to think of the future as well, for with my fortune assured I had no need to fear the Stranger and his vengeance. I could go where I pleased and send men to his door to chase him to the ends of the earth. How bitter those dreams soon were to become.

We came upon the city in the very midst of the forest one morning, not long after first light. One moment we were making our way through the jungle, unable to see anything through the foliage, and then it was there before us. Its seclusion was near total; only the thin trail that Diego had come across the day before even gave an indication that the jungle had any inhabitants at all. The walls of the city and the temples and palaces that loomed behind it were all recognizably Incan in construction, with their carefully fitted and shaped stones.

Diego stopped in his tracks at the sight of the city and began to tremble, his lips forming a soundless phrase that he kept repeating. It was something in his own tongue, which I cannot claim to understand. For a moment I feared he would flee and leave me to enter the stronghold alone, but instead he began a strange and hypnotic dance, chanting as he went. When he was through with his heathen display he set forth with his head high and his eyes proud. I followed behind, scanning the walls and the surrounding forest for any sign of a guard. There was none, nor had there been any sentries posted along the trail, which I found strange. Perhaps this place was so secluded that they had no fear of intruders happening upon it, but it still seemed odd they had taken no precautions.

The gates to the city were open when we came to them, and after idling a moment and waiting for someone to welcome us, we passed within. We found ourselves upon a vast avenue, which led to a grand temple that rose to the peak of the forest canopy at the city's far end. There were various other structures along the avenue—official buildings or temples of worship by the look of them. The street itself was empty, not a soul upon it, and none of the buildings we passed gave the appearance of being inhabited. Even the grand temple had the look of a thing abandoned, with grass and other jungle plants colonizing various parts of it. I glanced at Diego, who had a look of unease on his face, a feeling I shared. What had happened here?

As we came near the temple, a breeze stirred and I caught a whiff of smoke from a fire, the first sign of habitation that we had encountered. I started off down one of the byways, tracking this scent, Diego at my heels. We made our way through a warren of smaller streets filled with buildings set at odd angles, all overgrown with weeds and grass and in various states of disrepair. The smell of smoke grew stronger, and with it came the odor of meat roasting, which set our mouths watering instantly.

We hurried on, Diego rushing ahead of me in his excitement to meet his brethren. So it was that I heard his cry of dismay as the stench of death, hidden by the aroma of the roasting meat and the fire, reached my nostrils. I came around the corner to find him on his knees, head in hands, moaning in despair. Beyond him lay the meager remains of the last city of the Incas. I could well understand his desolation, for even I, who had no care for these people, was moved by the sight of so much suffering. Better to have fallen at Vilcabambe, I thought, than to survive and live and like this.

There were perhaps a dozen huts that were still inhabited within that city that must at one time have held ten thousand people, its grand avenues and temples teeming with people. That time had been long ago, it was clear. These were not the last survivors of this lost city; rather they had stumbled upon the ruins in their flight from the Viceroy's forces and had settled there, thinking to build a new civilization far from the Crown's reach. But though they had managed to avoid Spanish rule, they had been unable to escape the scourge that Pizarro had brought with him.

Nearly every man, woman and child there was ill with the pox. Looking them over, I thought it unlikely more than a dozen would survive. It had come upon them suddenly in the days before our arrival, as terrible and virulent as the plague that had taken my mother all those years ago. Diego wept even more grievously when he told me this after speaking with those who remained. When I asked him why, he said that it had to have been we who had brought it, for no one had left or come into their community since his brother had arranged to have word sent to him.

A terrible fate, to be the author of his people's doom. I mourned for Diego, even as he mourned for Julio, who had fallen to the illness the day before our arrival, and all the others who joined him in the days that followed. But as I helped poor Diego care for those who remained, my thoughts strayed to the future. It seemed obvious I could not stay here. There was no treasure and no gold, and soon there would be no one left. I had thought perhaps I could hide myself from the Stranger and avoid that terrible confrontation, but now I knew in my heart that it was not possible, though it did not stop me from trying. My next steps would set me on a path that led to you.

A MAIDEN'S HONOR

I MUST THANK you for the kindness you have lately shown me, though that may change once you have read all that I have written. At last you have relented in your ceaseless punishments and torture and have admitted that I am what I claim to be and no more. The truth is so simple and yet so hard to accept. Your women have borne witness to my womanly nature and you can deny it no longer. Have I not sworn to you that I will confess all? I shall demonstrate myself to be as good as my word.

After I left the Indians to their terrible fate in their ruined city I returned over the mountains, casting my way north until I found myself in Trujillo. It was an arduous journey, taking many months, during which I endured many trials that I will not dwell on here, for it has little bearing on the events that follow. After idling there for several days, and finding some luck at a gaming house, I bought passage on a ship headed for Panama. My fortunes turned while at sea, for the captain of the vessel, his heart overflowing with greed, weighted his holds with too many goods while at dock in Paita and the ship went down just beyond the harbor.

Only those of us able to swim made it back to shore alive. All my winnings had been put toward the passage, and so I now found myself stranded in Paita with no means of leaving beyond my own feet. This left me beset with worries, for I had wanted to take myself as far from the Viceroyalty as quickly as possible. I could only assume the Alcalde had pleaded his case with the Viceroy and others, making it dangerous for me to remain in Peru. The Stranger

95

was of even graver concern, for who knew to what lengths he would go to find me?

It seemed best, then, to go as far from Cuzco as I could manage. Yet I did not; quite the opposite. The reason for this was the boy Diego. He had followed me from that lost city, for—with his brother dead and seemingly everyone else soon to join his fate—there was nothing to keep him there. He hated me for what I had done to him, I am sure, but he had no one else in this world, and so he clung to me resolutely. I had tried to chase him away as I returned through the mountains, threatening to kill him and beating him with the flat of my blade whenever I could get my hands on him. In spite of that, he persisted in following me and, after a time, I gave up trying to stop him and we journeyed on together. I had even saved his life when the vessel sank in Paita, as he could not swim, having never been in water deeper than a creek bed.

It was on our third day stranded in Paita, as I tried to enact various schemes to gain us the coin necessary to make good our escape, that Diego attracted the attention of one Doctor Don Francisco de Idiáquez. The esteemed doctor was a professor of great learning from Vitoria who had fallen on difficult times and, as with so many of our fellow Spaniards, had fled the peninsula, seeking to find his fortune and settle his burdensome debts in this New World. He had settled in Paita, where he had worked for a time as a tutor to the children of the Rodriguez y Arce, one of the wealthier families in that city. Later he had gone into business with them and had made out well enough for himself that he now had one of the finer estates in town.

Don Francisco was about in the market when he caught sight of young Diego stealing some bread and seized him by the ear, demanding to know what he was about.

My master set me to the task, the boy told him miserably. We are without food or coin and he will not see to reason.

Hearing this, Don Francisco insisted that Diego bring him before me so that I could answer for what I had done. They found me in a gaming house, where I was trying to cheat at dice and my fellow players were about to turn upon me. One man had just called me a cuckold when the two of them entered the dimly lit room. Don Francisco interceded in our argument, telling the men that he would see justice done here, and took me outside. There he decried me for setting my poor servant to commit crimes that were the result of my failures as his master. After he had shouted at me for some time in the middle of the street and I had held my tongue, my ears burning with rage as I awaited a chance to free myself of this troublesome man, he suddenly shook his head and took a closer look at my face.

Why, you are no more a man than this boy, he said in disbelief. How did you become his master?

I am not, I said, I can assure. The boy has tied himself to me for reasons I cannot comprehend. His own people are dead, though, and he has no one else to turn to.

You should not abuse him so, Don Francisco said. No matter how dire your straits, we must set an example for the Indians, if they are to join us in the embrace of Our Lord and Savior. They are simple people and must be educated.

I allowed that this was true, but said that I was in no position to do so. I was little more than a boy myself, as the good doctor had noted, and I had to find my own way in the world, which was a hard enough a thing to do in this land without the burden of another to care for. I added a little of my own story, of how I had been wrongly accused of crimes and harassed and chased from Cuzco with only the clothes upon my back. This seemed to move the professor, and he embraced both Diego and me and said that we should accompany him back to his home where he would see to our needs.

He was as good as his word. We were fed and given a fine room to sleep in. The next morning Don Francisco took us both out and bought us new suits and boots, for ours had become ragged from so much travel and hardship. After, he brought us back to his estate and insisted that we remain with him for the duration of our stay in Paita. Though I tried to refuse his kindness, saying that he was far too generous to a rogue such as myself, he would not hear anything else, and the promise of a full belly and some time at ease beckoned too strongly. The boy seemed happy as well; the worry and anguish that had lined his face these past months vanished. His sleep passed uninterrupted by nightmare, a welcome change from those wearying nights when I would awake with him clinging to me, tears staining his face.

It was for Diego, then, that I elected to stay with Don Francisco, at least for a time. I owed him that much for all the suffering I had brought upon him and I thought, foolishly, that the Stranger and the Alcalde would be unlikely to find me so long as I remained within those walls.

The next three days were the first restful ones I had known since my time running Don Tadeo's shop. As much as I had thought I was staying for Diego's health, the truth was that I needed time to mend both body and soul as much as he. All those long days and nights under siege from the Alcalde and the Stranger, my flight over the mountains, thoughts of their pursuit forever shadowing my mind, had broken me in ways I had not even realized. To be able to sleep through the night, a deep and full sleep, without the worry of having to awaken at the first sign of trouble, was exquisite, worth more than all the food and clothes that Don Francisco could offer.

His generosity troubled me, though I pushed those concerns from my mind for a time, not wanting to tempt fate and thinking only to extend my stay as long as possible. Only rarely is something offered from the heart with no consideration given to a return in kind, though, so on my fourth day at the learned professor's estate I ventured to ask why he had shown Diego and I such kindness, when I clearly deserved so little.

The world has led you sorely astray, Don Francisco said, that an act of kindness must be questioned. Fortune has favored my days here in Paita, but in Vitoria I experienced many sorrows, including the death of my beloved wife. I know the cost to the soul of such hardship. I seek only to share that which has been granted me so that others might know the grace of Our Lord.

I accepted his words with a smile and some thanks—what else was I to say to someone who had been so generous?—but my worries still niggled in the back of my mind. I could not say why. Had it been Father Cardenado, or even Don Tadeo, who had said and done such things, I would not have doubted their intentions. With this stranger I was left cold, even in the warmth of his embrace. My instincts told me there was something false in him, yet there was no evidence I could use to justify this, as yet, inchoate feeling. Perhaps, I thought, it was just that my nerves had been worn by so many long months of flight that I now saw a dagger in every proffered hand.

We were not the only strays the professor had brought into his home; his estate was filled with young Indians and mestizos who did the work of servants in exchange for a home and some tutelage. He felt the great failing of our age was the lack of instruction of the natives in the ways of Our Lord, other Spaniards preferring to make their fortunes upon the backs of these poor souls. It could not be denied that the Indians of his house were well cared for, and had honest work to direct them. But they acted strangely, speaking only when spoken to by the professor, spending all other hours in silence. I saw no emotion cross their faces whenever I encountered them, though a few times I was certain I could see some cloud of turmoil forming in their eyes. It always vanished, the emptiness of their gaze restored to them, before I could be certain.

The eerie feeling they engendered within me seemed only to grow as the days passed, now five and then six, and still Don Francisco plied us with his endless honey. The more I watched the young men and women he was tutoring, the more like automata they seemed, following the same unchanging revolutions each day. Whenever I took to wandering the halls of the estate, or the surrounding grounds, I would see the same individuals occupied by the same tasks as the previous day at precisely the same time. After I first noticed this I studied them more closely and became convinced that their movements did not vary in the slightest from day to day.

Strangest of all was that no trace of any of them could be found at night. This I discovered when one night, as was often my habit when sleep failed me, I wandered the house, passing through any number of rooms that could have served as servants' quarters, only to find them all empty. In fact, but for the room Diego and I shared, the entire house was devoid of people. The chambers, which I assumed were Don Francisco's, contained not a soul, and the bed appeared untouched.

It was deep in the night by this time, the morning soon to touch the sky, and I feared that one of the Indian automata would stumble upon me in my wanderings, otherwise I would have investigated further. Instead I returned to my quarters, where Diego still slumbered peacefully upon the floor. Sleep did not return to me, and I spent a weary hour awaiting the cock's crow, my disquiet growing deeper by the moment. The next evening as I dined with the professor, our usual practice during this idle, I asked him about the servants.

They are very obedient and regimented, I said to him. You could conquer the Viceroyalty with them.

He laughed and said: The Indians are docile by nature, assuredly. They require guidance and a firm hand to reach their potential, otherwise they are given to sloth.

I asked him what potential that might be, and he told me that here he had ensured they achieved to the greatest extent of their ability, which was in their service to him.

Here they want for nothing—they are fed, clothed and educated in the ways of Our Lord and they do creditable work, he told me. So many of our fellows see only the gold to come, but I know the worth is in the man himself.

I understand your interest in Diego, then, I told him, for he has certainly been a wayward soul in the time I have known him. But an innocent in all matters of the world, needing only a guiding hand, as you say. But I fail to see what your intent is with me.

Don Francisco laughed and patted me paternally on the shoulder. The young never believe they have need of guidance. Do you not have much to learn of the world?

I allowed that this was so, though I was guarded in my admission, for the tone of his question implied that he was speaking of something very different from that of which he had been.

He smiled at my reserve, giving me an inscrutable look. I see how you are with young Diego, how he follows you everywhere and answers to your beck and call. He even sleeps at your feet like a dog. You govern him as I govern my Indians, do you not? I am just better at managing such things.

I had to confess that I did not know what the professor referred to.

Do not play the fool with me, he said.

He is overfond of me surely, I said, choosing my words carefully. But that is to be expected. I am the closest thing in the world he has to family. All that he knew of the world, all the laws that he assumed held true, crumbled at his feet, and now he must find his way amongst those ruins. It would drive anyone mad.

The professor nodded, pursuing the matter no further, though I could tell he did not believe what I had said. Nor did I believe him, for that matter, when he spoke of the Indians as children he was educating, for I had yet to see him teaching anyone. In fact, everyone I had seen seemed incapable of much thought beyond that required by the rigid tasks he had set for them. They were more dead than living, it seemed to me. I resolved then that I would find what became of the professor and his Indians in the night when he thought Diego and I safely asleep, for I did not wish to suffer their fate.

When I slipped out of my room it was deep in the night, well past second sleep, when not an honorable soul could be expected to be about in the world. I was at one with the shadows as I moved through Don Francisco's hallways, going from room to room, verifying again that all were empty of inhabitants. As I inspected what were ostensibly the servants' quarters more closely than I had the previous night, I was convinced that no soul ever lay their head upon those rough pillows. When I had satisfied myself that the house was empty, I turned to the grounds, scouring the stable where Don Francisco kept his horses, along with a few pigs and some cattle, finding no sign of anyone there either.

I returned to the house, convinced that I must have overlooked something there. A dozen Indians and a Castilian could not simply vanish into the air, even if the man was an alchemist, as he claimed. I retraced my earlier steps within, this time going slowly so that I could feel at the seams of the place, here at the floor, there at a fireplace, trying to find some secret passageway. None appeared, until I came to what appeared to be a newer addition to the house attached to the kitchens, which I had only glanced at on my earlier journey. At its far end, near where the entrance to the cellar was, there was an empty space, absent of purpose.

I went to it immediately, crouching down to run my hands along the floor, and was rewarded with the discovery of a trapdoor. I pulled it up and saw some wooden stairs descending into the inky blackness below. After checking to ensure that the door would not lock behind me, I went below. The darkness was near absolute, but I have always been at ease in the dark. When I came to the bottom of the stairs I could discern a pathway, carved from the earth and supported by timbers, as though it were the shaft of a mine. I half expected to be assaulted by the sound of pickaxes upon rocks and the searing stench of quicksilver, but the silence and the darkness held firm.

I started forward, the smell of damp earth heavy in my nostrils, unease tickling at the hairs on my neck. The farther I went the farther I was from my only avenue of escape, and the damper my palms and the drier my throat became. I walked for what seemed like hours, though in all likelihood it was only a few interminable minutes, the silence playing on my thoughts until my imagination had filled my head with any number of fearsome and terrible sights that I was certain were about to be revealed to me. The passage narrowed as I went until it came to a turn—somewhere near the edge of the professor's land, I reasoned—and after I had made the turn a dim light flickered into view at the end of this new tunnel. I slowed my approach, being careful to make absolutely no sound as I went, though I could hear nothing from the room where the light was.

I crouched low as I came to the entrance and peered around the corner, my body pressed against the cold earth. Within I saw a cavern, ancient and wide, formed long ago by the vagaries of the earth. I paid little mind to this wonder, though, for a far stranger sight drew my attention: all the professor's servants were arrayed in a circle upon the cavern floor, each of them with a vial attached to their arms. Studying them closely, I could see that these vials were being filled with blood dripping slowly from small punctures on the Indians' wrists. At the center of this nefarious circle was a goblet that, I knew without looking, was filled with blood.

I hissed at the sight of it, recalling the terrible rites the Stranger had been carrying out in the tombs of Cuzco. What foul necromancy was taking place here? I turned my attention to the poor Indians whose blood was being stolen, shaking the nearest to me to see if they were asleep. He did not rouse, and no breath seemed to pass from his lips. Had they somehow passed from the realm of the living and now inhabited some purgatory in this place? I was so engrossed in my study of the Indians, my own horror rising like bile in my throat, that I did not notice the shadows begin to move until it was too late. A firm blow struck my head and I fell to the ground and was lost to oblivion.

When I awoke, the light in the cavern had gone out and the Indians had risen, only the goblet remaining at the center of the circle. I was at the far end of the cave, my wrists and ankles chained to some ancient stone lodged in the earth. I had no idea how long I had been unconscious, but I suspected it had been some time and that morning would be near. Would Diego be joining me soon, I wondered? As if in answer to my thought, he appeared, led by Don Francisco. I called to him but he gave no sign that he heard me, his face blank of thought and expression.

A chill went down my spine at this sight, and my horror only grew as Don Francisco led the boy to where his Indians had so recently lain having their life force drained from them. He drew a thin knife from his belt that I could see was ornamented with oddly shaped runes, along with one of those fiendish vials of his. That he tied to Diego's wrist, muttering some phrases in Latin, the knife poised in his hand. He pierced the boy on each wrist, one draining into the vial, the other left to open to feed the earth.

Diego, you are not his, I called to him. You must resist him.

Don Francisco laughed at my words. He is yours no longer, he said to me, leaving the boy and walking over to me, a malicious look in his eyes. Soon enough he will be mine, as docile as all the sheep in my flock.

I spat on the ground at his feet, cursing his name. What of me, I said. Do you expect me to be transmuted into one of your automata?

No, he said. Your kind does not respond well to my treatments. I have other plans for you.

What are your plans for the boy and these others, I asked, my fury growing by the instant. Are they to be drained until they are husks. I thought you were educating them and turning them into Christians.

Indeed I am, the professor insisted. Christians and good subjects. They are obedient and observant, not the slothful and ignorant sort like your boy here. He will learn his place in time.

Christians? I laughed at him. What claim do you have to our true faith? What foul rite are you practicing here?

Don Francisco looked at me scornfully. I am a philosopher and learned man and I will not have someone of your kind saying that I am not a Christian or a man. What you see here is no black rite, no foul magick, but a philosophic investigation into the most important alchemical secrets of our age. What I am collecting here is the divine quintessence of this land. This is the secret Magnus told Aquinas upon his deathbed, the secret to eternity itself.

As for you, he continued, stroking his chin with his fingers, a dear friend has requested that I keep you here. He is most eager to reacquaint himself with you.

My heart went still at his words and I felt myself begin to tremble. Though I tried to master my emotions they must have shown upon my face, for Don Francisco chuckled at my reaction.

Yes, I thought you would remember my friend. You are in his debt, as I understand it. You should know that he only accepts payment in blood.

I should not be surprised you would be in league with that devil, I cried, anger surging to overwhelm my fear. Do you do this work for him? He has worked his black magick on you as well.

Don Francisco scoffed at my rage. Don't be a fool, he said. He is one of the great minds of this new world. A philosopher of existence to rival Magnus. It was he who taught me the secrets of the philosopher's stone. But enough chatter, young Diego's vial is full and I have much to teach him.

He turned his attention to the boy, untying the vial and emptying it in the cup, which was now full almost to the brim. He fingered it tenderly, as though it were the holiest of grails, and then pulled Diego to his feet and began to lead him away. He paused before he left the cavern, as though a thought had just occurred to him, and turned to say to me:

Tell me, then, I am given to understand from my friend that you can survive for quite some time without food or drink. We shall see, at any rate.

His laughter, grim and cold, echoed down the halls of the passage long after he had disappeared from sight. I was unable to stop myself from snarling and cursing like a rabid dog at him, but as soon as the sound of his mocking had vanished from the air I started to weep, for the Stranger was now on his way from Cuzco, and with him came my doom.

It seems to be my fate to forever be finding myself imprisoned, chained and left for the dead. Even the convent was a prison, the walls and the veils forever shadowing my mind. Women, being the weaker sex, can perhaps submit to such things more easily than men, as can those of the plebeian classes, for docility has been bred into them over the generations. None of that is in me. Though it may be my fate, I have never accepted it. Even now my soul still cries to shake loose these bonds and roam again. For now, out of respect for you and what we have agreed to, I remain penitent and mild, knowing that you serve justice.

I spent two days in chains in the earth below Don Francisco's estate, without food or water, growing weaker with every passing moment. I knew I had to escape, for I dared not face the Stranger in in such a condition. He possessed more strength, aided by the foul magick he practiced, than I could ever hope to. It was only chance that I had survived our first encounter and trickery that had enabled me to avoid any others. He would not be easily fooled, I knew, so my only hope lay in somehow besting the professor before he arrived. That would be a trick in itself, for he would surely be on his guard, though perhaps he was arrogant enough to believe he had me cowed.

I considered shucking my bonds immediately—no mean feat, for the chains were bound tightly to me—but rejected it out of hand for the moment. There was only one exit from this terrible cavern and I assumed that Don Francisco would have it watched at all times. I had to also consider the matter of his magicked servants. They appeared docile and harmless enough, but I suspected that they would be capable of more. They were completely under the professor's command, after all.

Both nights that I was trapped below, Don Francisco returned with the Indians, including Diego, arranging them in his foul circle and draining them of their divine quintessence. The first night I cursed him for a devil, but he laughed and ignored me, leaving the Indians to fill the vials, returning only toward the end of the night to release his servants and fill the rune-covered goblet. The second day I changed my tack, pleading with him and asking to be initiated into the secret arts that he practiced. I tried to appeal to his vanity, praising his intelligence and the good that he had done for the Indians who suffered under his care, but he would not be persuaded.

After Don Francisco had left the Indians to fill their vials, I tried calling to Diego to see if I could summon him. He lay as if in the deepest slumber, his life force slowly dripping away. I entreated him throughout the rest of the night, speaking until my voice was raw, calling upon memories of our friendship and the trials we had suffered along the way, hoping to stir something within his soul that would free him from the bonds Don Francisco had placed upon him.

It was all to no avail, and the next day, my third trapped below,

I despaired ever being able to see the sun again. Such was the state of my mind that I could do no more than lay down to sleep, the first time I had done so since the professor had chained me there. As soon as my head touched the earth I lapsed into a slumber so deep that I would have appeared dead to anyone who chanced upon me. During my quiescence I had a dream unlike any other, in which I found myself staring down at my own body as I lay on the cavern floor. It was as though I had perished and my spirit had risen, but instead of ascending to heaven, or falling below to purgatory, I made my way back up the passageway to Don Francisco's estate.

I slipped through the trapdoor and above to the kitchen with ease, passing by the two automata set to guard it as though I were a ghost. I prowled through its hallways and found Don Francisco conducting lessons with Diego. Of those unspeakable rites I will say no more, except that I knew then that nothing I could do would bring Diego salvation short of death. The rest of the Indians went about their routines exactly as before. I approached several of them, whispering in their ears the very words that Don Francisco chanted each night at the conclusion of his foul ritual. They appeared to prick their ears at my words, though no sound emanated from my lips. With that I left them, my spirit returning below to my body, and I awoke.

My vision left me shaken; even now I am ashamed that I uttered those fearful phrases that passed so easily from the lips of Don Francisco. I told myself that it had been only a dream, my desperate situation giving terrible license to my imagination and that I should not trouble myself over it. Yet the dream had been so real, and part of me believed that my spirit truly had gone above to the estate and that I had witnessed and done all that my dream had shown me. Still, I knew that I could not spare any thought to that trouble, for greater worries were before me.

It had been over a week since I had come to Paita and been ensnared by the good doctor's ruse. No doubt he had sent word immediately to the Stranger, who, I could only hope, had remained in Cuzco. How long would it take for the message to reach him and how long would his journey to Paita take upon his receiving it? For any normal man I would have believed I had plenty of time to engineer an escape from my predicament, but these were no ordinary men and I would only grow weaker the longer I remained where I was. I knew I had to act while my strength was still with me.

That night I did. When Don Francisco arrived with his automata, including Diego, I was ready. I said nothing to him as he prepared his minions, and this drew his attention. When he finished with them he came to look me over, a curious glint to his eye. Satisfied that my chains were still upon me, he smiled and said to me: Are you broken already? I had thought from what my friend told me that you would still have some spirit left to you by the time he arrived. Perhaps not.

I said nothing, keeping my eyes downcast.

No matter, he said, he shall avenge himself upon you regardless.

He returned to the Indians, checking the vials again to ensure that all was well. I chose that moment to act, shouting out the words of his infernal ceremony and, by some miracle of Our Lord, the very Indians that I had whispered the words to in the spirit form of my dream rose to their feet and turned upon the professor. He gave a shout of rage and commanded them to lie upon the ground. For a moment it looked as though they would obey him, all of them halting where they stood, a look of confusion crossing their faces, but I uttered his spell again and they fell upon him, striking at him with a tremendous fury.

Don Francisco fought against them, trying to use his spell to turn the automata aside, to no avail. Their strength, now unleashed, proved too great and he quickly fell under their blows, crying out in agony and fear. While this took place I did not waste a moment, working at the locks on my chains until I had slipped free of them. Seeing this, Don Francisco cursed me, but the melee he was at the bottom of did not allow him to stop me.

I fled past him, going first to Diego to see if I could loose him from the professor's bonds. I called his name and uttered the words that I was convinced would unlock his soul. He did not rise and, in fact, gave no indication that he had heard me. I crouched beside him, staring into his eyes and, though he returned my gaze, no recognition passed across them. Behind me I could hear Don Francisco trying to regain command of his minions, and I knew I could not linger, so with tears in my eyes I stood and left Diego to his fate.

Before I left the cavern I spilled the goblet, sending the blood to the earth for it to absorb. Don Francisco cried out in anguish as he saw me and threw aside the last of the Indians I had set against him, starting for me. I fled down the dark passageway, the professor at my heels, until I reached the ladder and the trapdoor. I was up the ladder and had flung the door open to go above when Don Francisco seized my ankle, pulling me down below.

I caught one of the rungs of the ladder as I fell, and clung to it, even as Don Francisco snarled and pulled at my feet. Struggling fiercely, I managed to get one leg free and struck at him with it, landing a few blows upon his head. He was relentless, though, refusing to let go, and finally he managed to grasp my free leg and reached up to seize my belt, and began to pull me down. Rather than struggle against him further, I let go of the ladder, pushing off hard, so that we both tumbled down. I landed upon his chest and he let out a gasp and lay stunned upon the ground.

I left him there, ascending the ladder again, free of entanglements, slamming the door shut behind me. Casting about, I found a heavy cabinet in the kitchens, and with all my strength I pushed it over the trapdoor, sealing Don Francisco within. I waited a moment until he had regained his senses and climbed up to test the door. When I had satisfied myself that he could not dislodge the cabinet, I left him to scrabble against the door and went to his stables, where I saddled his finest horse and rode into town.

Perhaps you will have heard of the illustrious Don Francisco, for you are a learned man and I have been told that he wrote many treatises on the Indians and their nature. Of their quality I cannot speak, and I have no doubt that he is a philosopher and alchemist of the highest regard, for he showed me some of his art, but still I tell you he was a devil. His academy robes were but a mask, the same with his writings—his true face he revealed to me in the cavern where he chained me. All of us have many faces that we show the world, though men of honor do not admit to such things, but I have known it well in my journeys. Honor is but gold and the hand at the throat to keep those beneath you bowing and scraping before you.

I have little doubt Don Francisco escaped the prison I had trapped him in and regained control of the Indians he had bespelled. I did not desire his death, though surely he deserved such a fate, I merely wished to make good my own escape, and with him otherwise occupied I was able to. I rode into Paita and sold the horse, a fine beast, for 3000 reales to a fellow Basque. With my newfound wealth I bought passage on the first ship leaving harbor, bound for Lima.

Upon arriving in the city of my birth I considered setting sail again immediately, but I knew that any ship heading north would dock at Paita, and I did not wish to risk being entrapped by the professor again. I could hardly stay in Lima, though, for what if my father or one of our family's friends happened to recognize me as I wandered its streets? To the east lay Cuzco and the Alcalde, which offered no better options. As I was casting about for a direction, someone told me six companies were being raised for a campaign in Chile. I presented myself and enlisted as a private soldier, and in a week had departed.

I spent three years in Chile battling the savages there for the Crown. Of my time there I will say little, for it has no bearing on the story you wish me to tell. I was raised to the position of lieutenant in our company for my service in Valdivia, where I suffered three arrow wounds from the Indians who attacked that town. It was difficult work there, but I enjoyed it, for the Spaniards there were warm and welcoming, all of us sharing in the miseries of our daily toil against the Indians. I might have stayed there much longer had I not encountered some difficulties with the captain of our company.

He was a good man and, after my exploits in Valdivia, he had treated me as a son, providing me with much sound guidance. The trouble came because of a woman, I am sorry to say, that he saw quite regularly in Concepción. He invited me a few times to her house, where we all shared wine and game. But, fool that I am, I could not leave well enough alone and I took to visiting her when he was not there. I am not sure how I drew his suspicion—perhaps the woman said something—but one evening he followed me on my way to call on her and confronted me. Words and insults were exchanged and a duel resulted. He pressed me hard and I was forced to run him through to preserve myself.

With my captain's death I knew there was no possibility of my staying any longer. The governor of the place was a hard man who favored my captain and held no esteem for me, so I knew I would not be fairly judged, though I had killed the man in self-defense. I called on my friend Don Pedro de Aillon, a captain of another company in Concepción, telling him what had befallen me and begging him to help me. He agreed that it would be best if I left that city, and so he gave me some arms, a little food and water and a horse, and sent me on my way.

It was a terrible journey. That I survived is only due to the providence of Our Lord. I went along the coast initially, thinking it would ease my travel. I found nothing but desert there, barren of people or sustenance. For the first two days I saw only a few Indians, who fled at the sight of me. On the third, I encountered two Spaniards, deserters like myself, who said they were trying to reach Tucumán. I threw in my lot with them and we pushed on into the mountains. They were even more desolate than the land we had just come from, if such a thing were possible, so all of us despaired our fates. I kept my hope, recalling my journey with Diego across those mountains, which had been no less forbidding than these.

There was so little to sustain us—only a few meager roots and herbs with no animals to be seen—that we had to kill our horses, one by one, to survive. Little good it did us, for by the time it came to kill them they had been reduced to little more than gristle. There was nothing for it but to press on, hoping that we could find some measure of civilization before we all perished. We reached such a state in those fearsome peaks that we were unable to start a fire, so addled were our minds by hunger and thirst, and so we spent several frigid nights keeping each other awake so that we did not perish in our sleep.

Madness seemed to touch us all in the days that followed, so certain were we that our lives were at an end. I am hesitant even to write of it, for my memory of that time is clouded. One of the men I traveled with, who called himself Juan de Silva and hailed from Santiago, accused me one day as we stumbled along of concealing food from the two of them.

I reacted with fury to his accusation, saying: How could I have done so? And when would I have had to opportunity to find any? We have been together every moment of every day.

But not at night, the other man interjected. His name was Alonso García Remón, an ugly man of low character. He added: I have awakened at night to find you gone and when morning comes you have returned. All without a sound, as if you had flown off like a bird.

What nonsense, I said. Even if I was capable of such a feat, there is no food nearby. We have exhausted ourselves searching for it. And if I could simply fly away and off this mountain, do you not think I would have abandoned you long ago?

Alonso spat on the ground at my feet and said: I have no doubt you would abandon us if you could, you cur.

I cursed the fool and made to draw my sword, but Juan stepped between us, speaking in a soothing tone so that the only result was that Alonso and I avoided each other's company for the rest of the day. I stayed to the front of our group, breaking the trail, while Alonso and Juan followed some paces behind me. They stayed far enough back that they thought me out of earshot and they spent the afternoon whispering to each other. Each time that I glanced back to ensure they were still following me, they halted their discussion and would not meet my eyes. I said nothing, pressing forward, my only thought on surviving this ordeal.

That night, as we huddled together for warmth, our breath clouding the air around us, the stars and moon of the heavens our only witnesses, the two of them seized me by the arms and pinned me to the ground. I struggled fiercely against them, kicking and shouting, calling on the Holy Virgin to save me. They laughed at my words, landing several blows upon my head that left me stunned, and proceeded to conduct a search of my person. When it revealed nothing they both stalked away in the darkness, muttering and cursing to themselves.

Have I proven myself to you now, I called after them. Are you willing to stand before me as men, or will you just slink away like knaves?

They did not return that night. I slept for none of it, fearing that at any moment the two scoundrels would return and fall upon me. By morning I was fatigued beyond measure, my nerves so frayed I could not even steady my hands. I forced myself to strike out, for I dared not linger while the two of them were still about, no doubt waiting for a chance to attack me again. My pace was unsteady, for my exhaustion was at its peak. There were times when I am certain that I slept as I walked, and my thoughts were haunted by visions of food and warmth, hearth and home.

I came across the two of them later that day as I descended from the mountains into a valley filled with scrub and brush, a veritable feast of vegetation. I scrabbled among the earth for a time, pulling free a few roots that I began to chew upon as I walked, ignoring the fiercely bitter taste of them. I exulted as I went at this sustenance, no matter how scant and foul it was. I had just finished the last of it when I crested a small rise and saw Juan weeping over Alonso's fallen body below me. Forgetting our troubles of the previous day, I ran toward them both, calling out and asking what had happened.

Juan glanced up from his fallen companion, a look of terror crossing his face at the sight of me. You have murdered him, he cried out, backing away from me.

This enraged me beyond measure. Traitor, I yelled at him. After all that you have done to me you accuse me of betraying you. I should run you through right now.

He fell to his knees, raising his hands before him as though to plead for his life. Forgive me, he said, we treated you wrongly and deserve whatever punishment the Holy Lord decides for us. I will do what you wish, but do not strike at me as you did him.

What are you talking about, I said to him. I have seen neither of you since your betrayal last night and you accuse me of murder?

I do not know how, Juan said, beginning to weep again, but his was not natural death. We were walking along, happy to be in the warmth of this valley, when he fell to the ground, unable to draw a single breath. Though I did what I could to aid him, it was no use—he suffocated. And now you appear, just as he perishes. It surpasses all reason.

Listen to yourself, I said to him earnestly. How could I kill a man when I was nowhere near him? I am not some alchemist who can transmute the air.

No, he said, you are far worse. You are a spirit. The devil himself is your ally.

I strode forward and seized him by the shoulders, shaking him so violently that he cried out. I said to him: If I am a spirit, the devil's familiar, then how did you and Alonso seize me last night? You could have killed me then. By the grace of Our Lord you did not, and for that I am thankful. All this time without food, and this endless march, have driven us all to precipice of madness. Can you not see it?

He shook his head and pressed his eyes closed, his lips working silently in prayer, as though he might will me away. Disgusted, I pushed him to the ground and stalked away. As I went, I looked over my shoulder and called out to him: Come with me or you will share his fate! Enough of this madness. Do you think you can survive the rest of this journey on your own? We must go together or perish.

Juan did not raise his head from where he lay, and for a moment I thought he had joined Alonso in death. At last he stirred and crawled over to where his fallen companion lay, not once looking in my direction. I turned my back upon him, abandoning him to his fate, though I was convinced he would perish. My own life, too, I felt was at stake if I remained in that place much longer. As I walked on I was so overwhelmed by emotion that I wept bitterly and was barely able to go on. After a time I recovered my senses and, after commending my soul to the Holy Virgin, I continued on with a clear mind. I could only pray that my journey would soon be at an end.

It was the next day, or the perhaps the one following, that I was saved. I cannot recall; my senses were too deranged from exhaustion and hunger by then. My boots had worn away and my feet were bloody from walking, my clothes but rags. What a sight I must have been! I had walked until I could go no farther and then collapsed upon the ground, propping myself up against a tree so that I might see if somebody chanced past. I primed my arquebus so that I would be ready to fire if need be, though I feared I would not be able to lift the weapon.

Fortune stood by me that day, for I was not far from a trail used by the locals of the area, and two gentlemen happened upon me not an hour after I had fallen. It seemed that I had somehow found my way near Tucumán and, though the region I was in was barely inhabited, there was a ranch not far away. Those fine men, seeing the deplorable condition I was in, set me on one of their horses and took me to that place to see if they could spare a bed. Though I could hardly speak, my lips and mouth so dry they bled, I thanked them both profusely.

The ranch was run by a mestiza woman, a stern widow, whose expression immediately was softened when she saw my pitiable state. She had me put in bed and nursed me to health with soup and a bit of wine. I was near delirious, raving to her about the trials I had suffered, while thanking her for her kindness. She soothed me and told me to sleep and regain my health, that I could have a bed for as long as I needed. I slept well into the next day and when

I finally stirred I saw that there was a woolen suit and some boots set out for me to wear. Shedding my rags and putting these fine gifts on, I went out to find my benefactress and thank her.

The Widow possessed untold numbers of cattle, horses and other livestock, all collected on a vast ranch. Compared to myself, she was wealthy beyond all imagining. When she saw that I had risen from my bed and that my health had somewhat returned to me, she sat me down and inquired as to how I had come to be in such a state. I gave her some tale about having become lost while on a journey, giving her to think that I had simply been traveling this region and had been badly mislaid. I think she had her doubts in what I said, if I were to judge by her expression, but she did not press me on the matter.

In spite of whatever misgivings she may have had, the Widow let me stay in her home for as long as I needed to recover from my trials, for which I was exceedingly thankful. In return I offered her what help I could, while pondering where I should go next. My eagerness to assist helped to warm the Widow to me and to take her thoughts from suspicions about my origins. Where had I come from and why had I ended up on the edge of nowhere near death? There was no answer that put me in a kind light, which both of us knew, so I could only hope my hard work shone brighter.

One evening after we had dined, for the Widow insisted that we always dine together, we retired by the fire to share some brandy and talk. This was her usual habit, one for which I was glad, for I learned a great deal of Tucumán and of her on these occasions. On this evening she sat nearer to me than usual, taking me by the hand and thanking me for all I had done for her. You seem to enjoy the work here, she said thoughtfully.

It has been a great restorative, I agreed. And it seemed the least I could do with all that you have done for me. I would not make myself a burden to you.

You have been just the opposite, she said. I admit I had my doubts when I first saw you. I thought you little better than a criminal, for that is who seems to so often pass through these parts. But you have proven yourself honest and a hard worker.

I am glad that I have earned your trust, I said to her. I hope that I prove worthy of it.

As do I, she said in a tone of voice that caused me to glance at her. Her smile deepened as she held my gaze, and her expression was at once both a challenge and an invitation.

As I wondered at the cause of this, she said: I am looking for a suitor for my daughter. It must be someone who is suitable, a Spaniard obviously, of an honest disposition and who is willing to remain in a place such as this. Am I wrong in thinking you such a man?

You overwhelm me, I told her, with your consideration. I am utterly undeserving of such a reward, especially after all you have already done for me.

We shall see in fact whether you are deserving, she said to me in a mischievous tone. A testing is in order.

How does one find the measure of a man, I said to her, matching her tone.

I have my means, she said, laughing. Taking me by the hand, she led me away.

I am hesitant to write of the days that followed, for now I have nearly reached that moment in my tale where you arrive upon the scene. I do not fear for myself. I have been open with you in my confessions, though you have doubted the truth of them time and time again. But I will suffer the consequences without question, for I accept my fate. What I cannot accept is that those dear friends who aided me in my hour of need should come to grief because I have mentioned them in passing in this chronicle. I could never forgive myself that.

Shall I try to extract some promise from you that no harm will come before putting ink to paper? Or do I assume that your more benevolent attitude of late extends to those I am about to write of? Hard choices, these. If you should put them to the screws to determine the veracity of what I have said...but I cannot think of it. Understand that they have done nothing wrong and that if crimes have been committed it is I who bears the responsibility.

After two weeks upon the Widow's ranch, which I spent hard at work, proving to her that I was an honorable gentleman, she announced that we should go to Tucumán to call upon her daughter and make arrangements for our betrothal. I gave her to understand that this too was my heart's desire, though, in truth, I had no interest in remaining upon her ranch for the remainder of my days. After all the days I had spent in her company I saw well how things would go following my marriage. I would find myself scurrying under her hard gaze, no longer the master of my own life and a stranger to my own bed. Some men may be satisfied with such a life, but not I—I have always yearned to wander, and I saw no need to stop now.

You will think me a scoundrel, and perhaps I am, but at least I am one who is honest with myself. I am under no illusions about my sins and flaws. Have I ever tried to hide them from you? You accuse me of wearing many masks, but my face and my honor have always been visible for any who chooses to see. Better to abandon a woman than to remain and betray her in my soul every passing day. But you know nothing of the corruption of the flesh other than what is in your books. There is much more to the world than can be found in those volumes. I should know, for in the convent I lost myself to them until I decided to taste such experiences for myself.

The strangest thing happened when we arrived in Tucumán— the Widow did not take me straight away to see her daughter, as I expected. The girl was apparently staying with some friend of the family, while we stayed at the Widow's home in the city—an arrangement that seemed quite odd to me, though I suspected it was so she could keep me for herself for as long as possible. She continually made excuses as to why she could not introduce me to her daughter, claiming that she had much business to conduct before a wedding could take place, as she needed to ensure that her daughter's affairs were properly in order. Yet she continued to insist that we come to some formal agreement, in writing, as to the betrothal. Here I found excuses to delay for, as I told her several times that I could not in good conscience become betrothed to a woman who had not pledged her heart to me.

That is of no consequence, the Widow said to me each time I equivocated. I am the girl's master; she will marry as I say.

Still, I said, it would set my heart at ease to see the girl before we embark on such a journey.

We would go back and forth like this, trying to ensnare the other in some trap, until one of us would storm off angrily, saying that the other could simply not see reason. Yet later that day or the next we would always find each other and begin again. I believe the Widow enjoyed the challenge I represented and took great pleasure in the arguments we shared. I know that I did. It was a strange kind of seduction we were about, where I played the woman, always demure and unwilling to give up her guarded treasure, and she played the man trying to find the Traitor's Gate to my citadel.

No doubt she believed that eventually I would succumb to her demands, for she knew I had little in the world beyond my honorable name, and she offered me a fortune for my servitude. I certainly gave her to think that I would, even as I plotted my own escape. In the meantime, I saw to my own needs, for the Widow, when she was not doing battle with me, left me to my own devices, preferring that I not be involved in whatever business she was conducting. This should have roused my suspicions, but I was only too eager to take advantage of the opportunity to acquaint myself with what gambling and drinking houses there were in this fine city.

During one of my sojourns in a gaming house run by a fellow Basque, I encountered one Don Rafael López de Arguijo, a name you will well recognize, given that he is your confidant, as I now know only too well. He took an immediate interest in me, especially after I had told him something of my background, and invited me to dine with his family on several occasions. I went, though I had to be careful that the Widow did not grow suspicious of me, and after several days Don Rafael confessed his reason for his befriending me. He had a niece who needed to be married, and he thought I would make a fine match.

I can attest to the girl's virtue and her father's honor, Don Rafael said to me, and she has a fine dowry.

I am hardly deserving of such generosity, I said to him.

You would be doing me a favor as well, he said. The girl needs to be married and there is not a suitable match in town for her. If you are willing, I can arrange a meeting and we can see it done.

I agreed, and three days later, after making my excuses with the Widow, I called upon the Arguijo household. There I was introduced to Francisca, the niece of whom Don Rafael had spoken of. She was an ugly thing, far contrary to my tastes. With her was Don Rafael's daughter Mariana, a plain-faced girl with a spark in her eye that drew my immediate interest. I spoke to both of them for much of the evening, under Don Antonio's watchful supervision, praising Francisca for her grace and beauty and regaling them both with tales of my various adventures. This pleased Don Rafael greatly, and when the evening was done he spoke to me with great excitement about the betrothal, which he considered a fait accompli. I agreed that all seemed well, but asked for some time to settle some matters before I committed further, which he agreed to, though reluctantly.

Imagine his anger if he had realized that my every word to Francisca was intended for Mariana's ears, a fact I made plain to her with several veiled and significant glances. That she realized I had no doubt, for she responded with sly smiles of her own, managing once to brush her hand against the back of mine as she refilled my glass with wine, while poor Francisca and Don Rafael were none the wiser. The clever girl also orchestrated a brief meeting alone between the two of us before the evening ended, sending herself to get some more wine and then calling for my assistance. She was waiting for me down the hall from where Don Rafael had received me, just beyond his sight.

Speaking aloud, so that the others might hear it, she thanked for my assistance and then added with a bold smile: I have never had occasion to meet so fascinating a person. Then she seized my hands and pulled me close, pressing her soft lips to my ear.

You have brightened my dreary days, she whispered to me in a voice hardly louder than a breath. I am so often left alone here with nothing to pass the time.

She released me just as her father came to see that all was well and, smiling, she went to kiss him on the cheek and congratulate him on finding such a man as I for Francisca. He was well pleased, as was I, for I knew the meaning of her confidence. I resolved to call upon the Arguijo house again at a more favorable hour. Little did I know that act would set me upon the path that led to you and my doom.

The next day, as I prepared my excuses for the Widow so that I could assure myself of an afternoon spent at my leisure, she confronted me, demanding that I marry her daughter that very afternoon. She was quite impassioned on the matter, which gave me pause. I reminded her that, while I was naturally willing to go through with the affair, I could not in good conscience marry a woman whom I had not met and who, for all I knew, was being coerced in the matter. She did not like my implication and slapped me across the face. It took all my strength not to strike in her in turn, but though my face turned red with fury, I kept my passion in check.

Why, I cried in an aggrieved voice, should I suffer under your blows when you ask me to do what no honorable man would ever agree to?

She began to weep and apologize, taking me into her arms. I am sorry, she said, it is my fault that I have asked so much of you. If you could only understand. And now I fear you will run away from me. For I see how you make excuses and run off to play, as any young gallant would. Each day I ask myself, will he return? And I do not know.

I took her by the hands and looked her in the eyes and swore to her that I would never think to leave. We have grown so close, I told her, I cannot imagine anything that would make me happier than to be brought into the embrace of your family. You need have no fear; I will marry your daughter and be joined to you heart and soul.

I could see the doubt upon her face, the wound in her eyes, and yet when she released me and said that we would speak of this further that evening, I happily agreed and went upon my way. What a fool I was! I should have known that so strong a woman as the Widow would never give in so easily. But I thought nothing of it, my mind already casting ahead to the frivolity that awaited me that afternoon.

I sauntered about the streets of this city as though they were mine for the taking, making a great display of myself, before heading to a gaming house where I had, in the past, whiled away a day in those vain pursuits. This, I thought, would provide me with an alibi should one prove necessary, for I was not so much of a fool as to completely disregard the Widow. I thought it likely she had spies about, looking to see how I spent my days. How right that instinct proved to be, and how bitter that I paid it so little mind.

After spending an hour or to at cards, I slipped out of the place, taking care that no one noticed me, and went out upon the streets. I wandered for a time, straying far from my intended destination, crossing my own path several times, while halting here and there, to ensure I was not being followed. These precautions taken, I made my way to the Arguijo household.

Mariana was keeping watch upon her street, and as soon as she saw me, she set the servants to some task to distract their attention and let me in. We secluded ourselves in her sitting room and passed a delightful afternoon together, sharing whispered confidences so as not to attract the attention of the servants. Mariana told me that she wished that her father had offered me her hand in marriage, and I said that I felt much the same. This overjoyed her to hear. It seemed that Don Rafael was something of a tyrant and that no man could measure to his standards when it came to his daughter. She feared ever escaping from his watchful gaze. Both of us tried to think of some means to free her from his grasp, and I promised that I would help her in whatever way I was able.

You will laugh reading my words, no doubt, for this is not the tale Don Rafael gave you. But why should his oath carry more weight than mine? I will admit that talk was not all we did to while away the hours and, in fact, I became so distracted I did notice the lateness of hour, otherwise I would surely have left much earlier than I did. Likely that would have spared me, for no one would have been the wiser. Instead, I was still in his house when Don Rafael came home. He found Mariana and I reclined and frolicking together, our legs and clothes entangled.

It must have looked a sight, and he did not give me the benefit of the doubt, letting out a roar and charging at me with his sword drawn. I dashed from Mariana's arms in an instant, heading straight out the nearest window, before Don Rafael's blade had a chance to touch me. As soon as my feet touched the ground I fled into the city, hoping the coming darkness would obscure me. Behind me I could hear Don Rafael in mad pursuit, cursing and calling upon all of Tucumán to seize me, for I was nothing more than a scoundrel who had ruined his daughter's honor.

My only thought as I fled was that I could not return to the Widow's house, nor could I go to any of the gaming or drinking houses that I usually frequented, for Don Rafael would be familiar with all of them. The churches of the city were sacrosanct as well, for Don Rafael had mentioned his friendship with you. It seemed best to cut my losses and leave the city as quickly as I could, for the Widow would surely hear of this incident and Don Rafael would ensure that all other doors were closed to me. Fortunately I had kept my boots on with the sweet Mariana, as well as most of my clothes, though they were in utter disarray, making my headlong flight easier.

I ran until I had no breath to go farther, my lungs burning, my legs on the verge of collapse. The sounds of pursuit grew nearer and nearer. Don Rafael had apparently roused some confederates in his passage, for I heard the shouts of several others mixed in with his angry cries. The sun had nearly disappeared beyond the horizon, and for a faint moment I thought I might be able to use the coming darkness to cloak myself, but then I saw the mob come upon me with torches lit and in hand.

As it happened I had halted in the middle of a small square beside a fountain with a statue of Our Holy Mother. There was a small church at the far end of the square, and I knew I would have to flee there, even if it would only delay my inevitable capture. That seemed preferable to being run through on the streets, as seemed very likely at that precise moment. I walked to the statue of the Holy Virgin, touching her marble robe, and offered a quick prayer, asking her to guide and protect me, before turning to face Don Rafael.

As they came into the square my pursuers slowed and, at motion from Don Rafael, spread out to cut off all avenues of escape, but for the church, which I slowly began to back towards. As I went I made a show of grasping at the hilt of my blade as though I intended to draw it and stand and fight. Seeing this, Don Rafael drew his own weapon and called me a coward and false-faced, demanding that I answer now for the dishonor I had done to his family.

I am a coward, I called out to him as I continued to back away, keeping a careful eye on his compatriots, trying to ensure they would not close the loop and seal me in their trap. You are the one who has half of Tucumán out with you. Is your honor so of such poor mettle that you need to call on that of other men to see that yours does not look tarnished?

What would you know of honor, you scoundrel? You have stolen the flower of my daughter's innocence, he snarled.

I have done no such thing, I said. She is as virtuous as she ever was. I came to call on you this afternoon, to thank you for all that you have done for me. You were not there, but she invited me in. We shared talk and nothing more, despite what you might think.

He laughed maniacally at my words and said: You expect me to believe that tale? You think your deceitful words somehow have a greater claim to reason than what my own eyes witnessed?

I do, I said defiantly. Everyone knows you guard your daughter jealously. There is not a man suitable for her in this town, if you are

121

to be believed. Is it any wonder that when you saw us together your reason abandoned you?

I saw that my words had struck home with some of the men with Don Rafael. A moment of doubt seized them and they paused in their advance. He could sense their questioning and turned, exhorting them that I was but a liar, deceitful to my very soul. Knowing I could wait no longer, I turned and fled toward the church, praising Our Lord that its doors still lay open. Don Rafael and the others, seeing me run, let out a cry and started after me. The moment seemed mine, for I was certain that I had enough of a start to the beat them to its doors.

In truth I did, but I was never to reach them. As I came near enough to see within the vestibule, a man stepped out beyond the sacred threshold, blocking my path. It was the Stranger, an ugly scar still marking his throat. His piercing blue eyes settled upon me as I came to a sudden halt before him, and he smiled.

THE EDICT OF SUPERSTITION

NOW WE REACH the end of my tale. If you have read to this point you will have realized just who the man I call the Stranger is, for he is no stranger to you. I know you still doubt me, and you will doubt what I have said of him as well. His scurrilous accusations have done me great harm, both in body and soul. He has bewitched you, just as he bewitched Don Lope and the others, and I know you feel the pain of that as much as I. Still, I have seen the look in your eyes and I know your doubts in me remain. Have I not told you the truth of my origins? Your women have inspected me and know it to be true, in spite of your attempts to accuse me of all manner of foul magicks. But enough complaints; I grow weary of these struggles.

There is little left to be told, though it contains the crux of my tale. If I have not proved my innocence of the absurd crimes I have been accused of by now, then what follows here should serve to set me free from your bonds.

It is impossible to describe the true depths of my feeling upon seeing the Stranger step forward from the darkness of that door to haunt my soul again. Was I never to be free of him? I was frozen before him, paralyzed by indecision and terror. Did I turn from the further defilement he would surely visit upon my soul and embrace the baying mob that wanted my blood spilt upon the square? I cannot lie, I did consider it. Better to embrace a quick death than the torture that I was certain awaited me at the hands of my sworn enemy. But the choice was not to be mine.

Before I had recovered myself, the mob, with Don Rafael at its head, fell upon me. In the melee that followed I was wounded several times, while landing a few blows of my own. Into the midst of this fracas stepped the Stranger, brandishing his rapier and shouting at Don Rafael and his compatriots to desist.

Whatever this cur has done to you, and I have no doubt it was a foul deed, he should stand before the authorities for his crimes, the Stranger said in a commanding voice that silenced the din around him.

He has dishonored me and my family and he will answer in blood, Don Rafael cried out, his eyes wild. I will strike down any man who stands in my way.

Some of the men who stood with him offered cheers of support, but the Stranger, standing tall above them all, was implacable in the face of their threats.

I would see this fiend answer for all his crimes, he said. I can assure you they are many and that it would be a kindness to him to be murdered in a vendetta upon the street. What of all the others whose cries for vengeance and justice will be in vain?

The men who surrounded us wavered, their blood lust tempered for the moment by the Stranger's reasoned words. Seeing that, he seized me by the shoulder, lest I try to escape yet again. His grip was so fierce that his fingers felt as though they were piercing my flesh. I cowered miserably beneath him, dropping my sword in surrender. Don Rafael, seeing me so reduced and cast so beyond hope, smiled grimly.

Let us finish him now together, he said to the Stranger. His dishonor demands an answer. Your blade can speak for whatever other crimes he has committed.

The Stranger shook his head and smiled. His blue eyes seemed to glow in the darkness, and I shivered as he cast his gaze upon me. I am afraid, gentleman, he said, that is impossible. I have no doubt that the injury to you has been great, but I can assure you that this is but minor incident when reckoned against all that he has done. He has committed crimes against Our Lord and he must answer for them.

There were murmurs from those gathered, and Don Rafael said: How would you have us proceed, then?

I am going to take this scoundrel before the Bishop this

evening, the Stranger said. As we speak, an Inquisitor is on his way from the Tribunal in Lima. The Bishop shall see that he is imprisoned, and once the Inquisitor arrives you will have ample opportunity to bring your charges against him.

This further quelled Don Rafael's ire. He said: You have spoken to him?

The Bishop? I have, the Stranger said. As soon as I became aware of this knave's presence in Tucumán I went to him, and together we wrote to Lima to call for an Inquisitor to be sent.

Knowing that he dared not defy his friend and confidante, Don Rafael relented, following in the Stranger's tracks as he dragged me through the streets. As we went I racked my brain as to what crimes the Stranger could possibly be referring to that would warrant the involvement of the Inquisition. While he might blame me for Don Lope's murder, or the deaths of some of his other allies, or perhaps even what had befallen the learned Don Francisco, the simpler course of action would be to remove me to Cuzco, where the Alcalde would gladly assist in seeing me punished.

There had to be, I told myself, some reason to involve the Inquisition, though it escaped me utterly. Of all the outcomes I had envisioned from that confrontation, this seemed to me by far the best. The mob had not slain me, nor had the Stranger, and, rather than keeping me under his own control, he was turning me over to the Bishop while he awaited the Inquisitor. Who knew how long it would take the man to arrive and, once he did, how long the investigation would take. It would be protracted, I would see to that, giving myself ample time, so I believed, to effect an escape.

I hardly recall the streets we passed upon in our journey to La Merced, I was in such a dread-filled stupor. Behind me I could hear the murmurs of Don Rafael and his compatriots as they discussed what the terrible nature of my crimes must be if someone from the Inquisition was willing to journey so far. If they could only have known the true nature of the man whose cold fingers burned at my soul as he clenched my shoulder. But it seems he has always been able to ingratiate himself among the honorable men of society, ensnaring them in his schemes and ensuring that his crimes go undiscovered.

The church was mostly dark, empty of all but one soul when we arrived. We did not go within, which I thought strange, but hovered upon the threshold waiting until a man stepped out to greet us. It was you, of course. I must say, my heart leapt at the sight of your kindly face, the genuine concern etched upon it, as you looked from the Stranger to the mob behind us, your eyes at last settling upon me.

This is the knave I spoke to you of, the Stranger said to you.

You nodded gravely and turned to Don Rafael: What is your concern in this matter, my friend?

This man has done grievous harm to my family and my honor, Don Rafael said. He has despoiled my only daughter, after I had shown him much goodwill and made him a good match with my niece.

I promise you that he shall answer for this my friend, you said. For now we must keep him under lock and key until the Inquisitor arrives. But I assure you there will be ample time for your concerns to be given voice.

I trust your judgment in this matter, Father, Don Rafael said.

And so it was that I was turned over into your care. Each moment I can recall with such clarity. The Stranger released me from his grasp, and I nearly fell at your feet to beg for mercy, for I had convinced myself that you—a bishop, no less—would be just and kind. You led me to your home, a palatial estate beside the church, where I was placed in a windowless cell. You ordered food and water to be brought to me and then smiled and said we would talk in the morning. The last thing I saw as you shut the door was the Stranger, his eyes staring at me as an animal does its prey, a knowing smile fixed upon his face.

Even after food and a candle were brought to me I could not shake that look from my mind. It seemed as though he were staring at me, even as I sat there miserable and alone. In some sense, I knew it was true. He would remain nearby so long as I was here, waiting for me to act. We both knew this game had only begun.

The next morning a servant brought me some food for breakfast and, after I was finished eating, led me to a well-appointed room somewhere within your estate, at the center of which was a broad table. The servant bade me sit in one of the chairs, which I did somewhat nervously. He left me alone and I cast my eyes about, wondering if I dared get up to investigate my environs. As I was just about to rise, he returned, bringing with him the Stranger, who sat across from me, an insolent glare upon his face.

You do not fool me capon, he said to me with a sneer. When I professed my ignorance as to what he was referring to, he scoffed at me. This act is wearing thin, he told me. You think I do not know what you are? After all that we have shared? The mask has long slipped from your face.

Even if I had forgotten, this—and here he pointed at the scar on his neck—would serve to remind me.

I do not have to apologize for defending myself from your depredations, I told him, refusing to meet his eyes.

If you think I have done you wrong, then stand against me capon, he said. Prove that your mettle can stand. How many nights did I await you in San Sebastián , looking in upon that miserable church as you cowered in fear, unwilling to answer for yourself as an honorable man? And still you pretend and you prevaricate. To the last. It will be your doom.

Those words chilled me, and I had to stop myself from shivering before the madman. He seemed utterly beyond reason at that moment, driven by some terrible lust I cannot give word to. It was not just what I had done to him, which was as a scratch is to any other man, or that I had done all that I could to avoid our next confrontation, but something about my very nature that he took as an affront. There is no other explanation I can find for his ire, which had grown out of all proportion to the wrongs, real or otherwise, I had done to him.

For some reason, this realization gave me heart. The Stranger was not some implacable being who could not be bent or turned aside once he had set upon his path. He was as petty and mean as any man. I determined to use this to my advantage.

You call me a coward, I said to him with a laugh. Who stood with the Alcalde and all his men surrounding San Sebastián, and who stood alone within? Who turns to the Inquisition and this kind bishop to do what he could not finish himself?

Your lies and trickery will get you nowhere within these walls, the Stranger said. There is only truth within here.

I am glad of it, I said. There is only one charlatan present.

He chuckled in a knowing way, which gave me pause. You and I are not only ones who will speak in the days to come. I would not sit easily if I were you.

My temper did me no favors then, for his insinuating tone got the better of me and I rose up from my seat and said to him: I await the day when I can finish the work I started there.

You chose that moment to enter the room, to my eternal regret, for my die was cast in your eyes from that time on. To you I was no more than a criminal and a fiend, as mean and petty as commonest of men. Everything that the Stranger had told you of me was proven true in that instant and I have never been able to show you the lie of it. You gave no hint of your feelings, though; I congratulate you on that. Your kindly visage remained firmly in place as you calmed and soothed the waters between us. I was comforted by what you said, believing your offers, and placing my trust in you, for I thought you were the only thing that stood between me and the Stranger. How wrong I was.

I tell you what follows, though you will know the incidents as well as I, so that you might know them from my perspective, and perhaps you will understand why I acted as I did. I do not know why such a thing matters to me now, after all that has passed between us, but I feel compelled to demonstrate that I have always been truthful with you. My honor demands it.

When you arrived you urged me to seat myself and said to me: Don Miguel has told me much of your temper and the calamity it has resulted in.

Is that what he calls himself here, I said. When I knew him in Cuzco, he went by another name.

Your imaginings hold no weight in this place, the Stranger said.

Please, my friend, you said to him, placing a hand upon his shoulder before turning back to me. I wanted you both here, as this is somewhat of an unusual situation. Unprecedented, even. Don Luis came to me several days ago, when word came to him that you were resident in Tucumán, and told me of the crimes of superstition and the practices thereof he supposed you guilty of. We agreed that the best manner in which to proceed with these accusations was to write to the Inquisition and have them send an officer to deal with this, for it is outside my jurisdiction, properly speaking.

I want to insist to you that I have cast no judgment upon you. It is for the Inquisitor to determine your guilt in these matters. If you should wish to confess your sins prior to that esteemed gentleman's arrival, all the better. I stand ready.

You paused for a moment to allow me the opportunity to throw myself at your feet and beg for forgiveness. I did nothing and remained silent, for my faith in Our Lord is unshakeable.

When I did not speak you nodded, as though in remaining silent I had told you all you needed to know, and you continued: Our predicament grows more complicated and unusual by the hour, though, for the Oidor has just sent word that a man has come forward accusing you of unspeakable crimes.

You had your eyes upon me, so you could not see the look of surprise and concern that passed momentarily across the Stranger's face as you spoke those words. I knew better than to ever take my eyes from that fiend, so I saw this instant of doubt seize him before it vanished, hidden beneath the placid visage he always assumes in your presence.

You continued: The Oidor has informed me he wishes to have you arrested to answer for these charges, which are most heinous. There is little I can do to deny him in this matter, nor do I wish to. However, should you confess to me now of your idolatry, your practice of magick and superstition, I can perhaps spare you the trials that awaits you at his hands.

I looked you in the eye and said: I will gladly confess to all my sins, but not these imagined ones.

You sighed and shook your head sadly, as though I were a wayward child who had ignored all your just counsel.

I have no choice, then, you said, but to turn you over to the Oidor. May the Lord have mercy on your soul.

Your words were intended, I think, to send a quiver through my soul, but I barely paid them any mind, for again I had been watching the Stranger and I could see his hands tighten upon the table as you spoke. Events were moving beyond his control, which could only be of benefit to me, and I do not deny that I felt some delight at seeing him at the mercy of forces beyond his command. I knew the feeling only too well, for it has ruled my days.

My happiness would have been greatly diminished had I known who my accuser was and what awaited me in the justice's hands. Perhaps I would have chosen differently in that moment, and perhaps our relationship might not have been filled with so much mistrust. As it is, we have always suspected the other of having knife at ready behind out back.

131

That afternoon the justice from the Audiencia, one Don Luis de Arellano, arrived and had me put in irons as both you and the Stranger watched. I was taken to the prison and thrown in a miserable cell and left there to rot for the rest of that day and the next two as well, with no word being give to me as to why I was being held. The prison was strong-walled and carefully built, and my cell was below ground, with only the smallest window granting me light.

At last, on the fourth day of my confinement, I was dragged from my cell and brought before the justice. He received me in a large room filled with the implements of his terrible trade. There was rack and irons ready for the fire, as well some other implements of torture, which I looked upon uneasily, for I knew they would not remain idle long. Don Luis was sitting in an ornate chair in a formal suit, while perched upon a stool at his feet was the notary who would be recording my testimony. He bade me stand before him as he looked me over, his distaste evident.

At last, having exhausted his study of me, Don Luis was moved to speak. He said to me: Do you wish to confess to those crimes which you have been accused?

I am guilty of no crimes that I am aware of, I said, staring straight ahead.

That you are aware of, Don Luis said. An interesting turn of phrase, that. I have the testimony of one Juan de Silva that suggests otherwise.

If he hoped to see me to react to this revelation, I disappointed him. I betrayed nothing of the surprise I felt at hearing that name. I had assumed the man dead, given the madness that had overtaken him during our last encounter. If he had survived, and it seemed he had, then I well knew what the accusations against me would be.

The justice, having given me my opportunity to confess, said: Juan de Silva has declared before myself, a notary and God that you traveled with he and another man, one Alonso García Remón, from Chile, where you had deserted from the army after murdering your captain.

Another pause, into which I interjected: It is true that I deserted, as did my two companions. We did travel together for a time, before they turned upon me.

Don Luis considered my answer for a moment before asking me: Do you admit to the murder of your captain as well?

I cannot deny killing him, I said truthfully, for it was my blade that cut him down. But it was not murder. We dueled over a woman. He felt that I had made him wear the horns and accused me of all manner of treachery, which I could not let pass without giving answer to.

The justice smiled thinly at my response, glancing down at the notary to ensure that all was being recorded. This seems a common complaint of those who make your acquaintance, he said. You are surrounded by treachery, yet never at fault for it. And all your dealings with women seem to end in sword play with their proper men, who feel they have been dishonored. I imagine that it is not your fault either.

Why should I bear the blame for men who are unable to control or satisfy their women, I said defiantly. I regretted it immediately, for a shadow passed over his face at my remarks. It seemed that he too was a friend of Don Rafael's, who, in all likelihood, had already begun to press his case with the Oidor as soon as he heard I had fallen into his hands.

His placid exterior restored, Don Luis said: It would seem you are blameless in all things. To return to the matter at hand. Juan de Silva has testified before God, myself and this notary that you did foully murder Alonso García Remón, and that you did so through trickery and other foul arts, in which you are well practiced. Not only did you murder Alonso García Remón, Don Juan claims you intended to murder him in order to feast upon their corpses.

I cannot deny that this accusation startled me, for while I had expected to be blamed for Don Alonso's death, I had certainly no expectation of being accused of cannibalism. Words failed me, and I stood rigidly before the justice and his notary, which he took as a sign of my guilt.

You fail to deny these accusations, he said to me, his eyes never straying from mine.

At last I was able to summon my tongue and speak, saying to him: I deny it most forcefully. Don Alonso certainly perished, but I was not present at that moment. In point of fact, both he and Don Juan had attacked me the night before, intending to kill me, and I just escaped with my life. When I encountered them both again Don Alonso had already expired, and Don Juan, driven to madness by his grief, accused me of his murder, though it was clear no hand had touched him. I was far away, and it was only happenstance I

133

came upon them.

How do you suppose Alonso García Remón perished? The question interrupted my unhinged babble, for panic had seized my heart and driven all coherent thought from my mind. All I could think was that I had to prove beyond any doubt that I was not a man eater.

I took a deep breath and stilled my thoughts, being careful to not look away from the justice. We spent many days traveling over hard ground in the mountains with little food or water, I said. No doubt he perished from the strain of the journey.

Don Luis pursed his lips and said: So you claim there was no murder, no trickery or magick on your part, that Alonso García Remón died of his own accord as a result of the strain of your journey?

Yes, I told him firmly. As I said, we all suffered greatly. The mountains are nearly impassable and certainly uninhabitable. It was only by the grace of Our Lord that I was found by some passersby and thereby saved. I was certain that Don Juan had joined Alonso and that I would be soon to follow them.

And yet you did nothing to help the man, he said to me, leaving him there to starve?

I begged him to join me, I said, shouting with anger. I begged him, but the fool refused. He would not listen to reason.

Don Luis fell silent as he studied me, raising a finger to his lips in thought, while I cursed my inability to keep my temper and wits about me. It was the suggestion that I was a cannibal that had so unnerved me I could not think straight, and led me to do the very things which confirmed his suspicions of me. At last he roused himself from his thoughts and said: So a man sitting on death's door refused your help? That does not speak well of you.

I began to protest but he ignored me, continuing to speak. I have heard enough of your lies. We'll see the truth pass from your lips yet.

At his words, as though the signal had long been prearranged, two men entered and seized me. Neither of them gave me so much as a glance as they went about their work, stripping me and tying me to the rack. When they had secured me to that gross implement, one of them left while the other assumed a position at the head of the device, ready to act at the command of the justice. Seeing that all was ready, Don Luis left his chair and began making a slow circuit around the device, his eyes upon mine. He appeared to be lost in thought, as though considering the matter at hand.

It took all my strength not to tremble under his gaze. That there was no glint of menace or pleasure in his eyes, which only made him all the more terrifying, for it was clear this was a task he viewed as a mere duty that it was his necessity to perform. I had never experienced such acts before, though I had heard enough from others to know that it would be a trial the like of which I had never endured. Yet my fate depended on my survival, so I summoned what courage and strength I had to brace myself for the coming onslaught.

The justice halted his circuit, standing somewhere above my head, just beyond my sight, and said in his calm voice: Did you foully murder Alonso García Remón?

I denied it, and Don Luis ordered the screw turned. His man set to it, and the bindings at my hands and feet tightened, my whole body following suit. The pain was agonizing. Each of the muscles in my legs and arms felt as though they were being torn asunder. Still, though I grimaced fiercely, I maintained my resolve and did not cry out.

Don Luis waited a moment to see if I had anything more to say. When I did not, he asked his next question: Did you foully murder Alonso García Remón, intending to do the same to Juan de Silva, with the ultimate goal of feasting upon their corpses?

I denied this as well, with a savagery that I think surprised them. It did not matter, for the screw was turned yet again. Now it felt as though all of my joints were about to come loose. An image seized my mind of my body, all its connective tissues having been rended apart, crumpled into a ball and tossed aside like a wasted piece of thread. It seemed impossible that I could endure even a moment longer, but still I held firm, my only reward a further turn of the screw.

I was determined not to give them the satisfaction of seeing me weep and beg for mercy, so with each question asked of me I proffered firmer and firmer denials in spite of the suffering I endured. I screamed many times as the screw was tightened further and further, and it seemed my body could no longer be pulled without giving way. How I endured such suffering I cannot say. Yet I remained whole and constant, my refrains unchanging, even as Don Luis repeated his questions, frustration beginning to edge his voice.

At last he abandoned his questions on the matter of Juan de Silva and Alonso García Remón and turned his attention to the accusations of Don Rafael regarding his daughter, asking me what I had done alone with her, implying that I had taken her by force. Here I made my first mistake, though I blame the duress I was under from the torture I was being subjected to. Instead of denying that I had done anything improper with the girl, I told him that she had invited me into her home and all that had followed, she had done willingly.

This admission drew a smile of triumph from Don Luis. He was about to continue with his questioning when a messenger arrived with a letter, saying that it was urgent. I watched the justice as he read it, his face slowly turning red with anger. When he finished reading he folded the letter up and I saw that his fingers trembled. He dismissed the messenger with a nod and then ordered that I be freed from the rack. He left the room without uttering another word or giving me so much as a glance.

I was given little time to wonder as to why I had been spared further punishment by the justice, for just as my limbs were freed from that terrible implement your secretary and two others arrived. He ordered his two men to put me in chains and have me returned to your residence. They had to carry me, one man under each of my shoulders, for my arms and legs no longer seemed to function of their own accord. No sensation emanated from them but for the pain that seemed to form another agonizing layer to my skin. It was its own being, clutching me in a smothering embrace from which I could not slip free.

Such was my state that I hardly noticed as I was returned to the room where you had first imprisoned me. They dropped me upon that hard bed of straw and locked me within, leaving me alone with the darkness and my discomfort. I slept on and off through the rest of the day, as much as the pain would allow, for every twitch resulting from my nightmares would shatter my oblivion, drawing me back into the terrible world I was trapped in. My thoughts were all half formed and misshapen, as though I were suffering under the spell of a fever. As a result, I could formulate no reason as to how I had been spared further turns of the screw upon the rack, nor how I had come to be in your possession again.

That soon became clear, for that evening one of your servants came again to rouse me and bring me into your presence. I found myself in the same room as before, though mercifully the Stranger was absent and the table was filled with food. You entered the room as soon as your servant deposited me in a chair, gesturing for me to join you and eat my fill. I was thankful for this gracious offer, though each movement was its own peculiar form of anguish. It was a struggle to merely to sit, so I was glad when you did not speak and we passed the meal in what must have seemed to you to be a companionable silence.

At its conclusion you turned your attention to me, fixing me with a kind smile. It has been a trying day, I'm sure, you said. I nodded, saying no more, and after a moment you continued: I have been made aware of Juan de Silva's accusations against you. They are most grievous and horrifying.

Again you paused and again I did not speak. You must have wondered why. There were simply no words left in me. I only knew that I dared not face the rack again, for I was not certain I could endure more than I already had. I admit that I was lost in these thoughts and that you had been speaking for some time before I realized and seized upon your words.

Of course such accusations are better handled under the court of the Inquisition, and so Don Miguel and I endeavored to have you returned to me until such time as the officer of the Tribunal arrives.

I nodded as though I understood, and agreed, and you took that as a signal to continue: It must be said that we need not wait for the Inquisitor to arrive. You paused for a moment as though considering your thoughts, and then put your hands together plaintively and said: Understand that I am not your enemy. I do not seek to persecute you, no matter what you might think. I pass no judgment upon you, I leave that to the Inquisition and Our Lord. I am here to help as best I can, as any servant of Our Lord must for his flock. But you are in difficult straits here and, from what I am given to understand, this is a not uncommon situation for you.

You paused again, and at last I was able to find my tongue and speak. It is not, I said. Trouble has a habit of following me.

You shook your head sadly and said: You speak as though trouble were a man who walked about on the very streets.

I stayed silent, though my thoughts were on the Stranger, who

137

even now I suspected was outside your home, keeping watch for me through the night.

But we are so often the authors of our own misfortune, you continued, especially those of us who go about their days with no humility before God. We must kneel before God, subject ourselves to His Glory and accept His judgment. That is the path of righteousness and it is a path free of trouble by our own hands.

I allowed that what you said was right and just, though in truth I still recalled Don Francisco's endless platitudes, all of which had proven false. I knew I could not trust you so long as you were allied with the Stranger.

I am glad that you agree, you said, and sighed as though a weight had been lifted from your shoulders. Now, I can help you. I must be honest, these are uneasy times in our fair city, and it is difficult to know where to place one's trust. The gentleman who came to me with the accusations against you, who has seen that the Inquisitor has been sent for, is someone who is not well known to me, though it seems you know each other well.

At the mention of the Stranger my mouth went dry and I found I could not look at you. Here I had so long feared that his hand would bring death with it, should it ever touch me, and instead I found only the long anguish of torture and imprisonment and the prospect of more to follow. This was infinitely worse than death, I realized, with every moment shadowed by the thought of him. It was as though I were awake in a nightmare from which I could not free myself.

Don Miguel—this was your name for him, though it is not his name; I will not write that word here—is a Visitor of the Crown here in Tucumán, you said. He arrived only two weeks ago, not long after you, if I am given to understand correctly. Since then things have been in something of an uproar, as you might expect. He is the reason you have been returned to me, for he has taken over the case from Audiencia, and for some reason he prefers that you face the Inquisition.

This drew my immediate attention, for it explained a great deal. Why did the Stranger seemingly have so many powerful allies spread across the entirety of the New World? No matter his unholy powers he could not so easily find pliable souls in positions of influence wherever he went. But if he was a Visitor of the Crown, sent to root out corruption in the Viceroyalty's administration, people like you would be far more willing to submit to his demands. The fact that he could summon an Inquisitor to this far-flung city demonstrated quite plainly that his influence extended even into ecclesiastical realms. No doubt there were things you would rather he not investigate with too fine an eye.

I allowed hope to enter my heart again, though it had been battered by the events of these last days, and I looked you in eye and said: What are you saying?

As I say, you told me, I do not hazard to know where the truth lies in such matters. I do not know that I can trust you, nor do I know that I can trust Don Miguel. He, I know, is hiding things from me. For he insists that you be held for the Inquisitor, but will tell me only in the vaguest way what he thinks you guilty of. Now this Juan de Silva arrives, a deserter and scoundrel if ever I have seen one. Rather than let the case proceed through the courts, Don Miguel takes it over, convinces young de Silva to cast his lot with him. It is all very strange.

You placed a great emphasis upon the last word, as though you thought I would understand what you meant. I nodded, for I well did. You sighed and stroked your chin, as though wrestling with some great decision, and at last, when the decision had been reached, you spoke again:

There are other rumors as well, other intrigues at play, and I must be very careful. I will not deny that I have my own petty stakes in this game, though I will not trouble you with those details. Suffice it to say that you are but a small part in the maneuvering that is taking place in this city under Don Miguel's watch. In spite of that, he places a great deal of importance upon your trial and he has placed you in my hands. Which means that I hold a very important card.

Me, I said with no little bitterness.

Yes, you said, I think that you know the cards are marked against you in this game. Don Miguel controls the Audiencia now; he could have seen your trial through to its end there. Yet he chose not to. I know you'll agree with me that this cannot bode well for you. Your only allies are time and, if you are willing to accept my help, me.

I studied your face carefully. I could detect no subterfuge there, though I knew that counted for little. At last, knowing I had no other options, I nodded and said: What do you propose?

Our only friend is the truth, you said. You have denied to me committing these crimes. Don Luis tells me you admitted nothing today upon the rack. He thinks you innocent in all likelihood, for he does not trust Juan de Silva any more than I. If you are innocent then the truth is what we require. I would ask that you write a confession, a chronicle of your days, if you will. I am not without my own influence, and if what you tell me demonstrates your innocence then I can perhaps keep you from Don Miguel's clutches. What do you say?

I asked to think on the matter for the evening, and you agreed. I spent most of the night that followed awake, my mind sorting through all that had occurred that day. In part this was because the injuries I had suffered at the hands of Don Luis still thwarted any attempt on my part to rest. But sleep would have been hard to come by in any event, for my mind was afire with what you had told me, as you had no doubt intended.

It seemed you were not the Stranger's ally, as I had assumed. But could I entrust my fate in your hands? If I did as you asked, there was nothing to stop you turning over my confession to the Stranger or the Inquisitor soon to arrive. The burden of risk was to be carried by my shoulders alone. I would be your pawn to be played as you so chose, sacrificed if it suited you.

I had little other choice, though, as you knew only too well. I was already in the Stranger's hands, for all intent and purpose, and I could not sit idly by awaiting my fate. You had given me an opportunity to shape my own future, to find a path out of this quagmire I found myself within. Who was to say if another chance would present itself? I had to seize it.

How strange it is to put ink to paper again after our last talk. To write of days that have not yet begun to fade from memory, as all days must eventually. Everything is still fresh and clear to me, each word, each expression, all my thoughts and feelings so vivid. This task, once so burdensome, now seems so easy compared to all I have endured. And its end grows near. One day soon you will unlock my door and lead me out to the sunlight yet again. There, I imagine we will embrace, thanking each other for all that we have done, and I shall go off into the world again. That day is not here yet, though, and so I will continue with what time is left to me.

The next day when one of your servants, a young girl named

Inés, brought me my breakfast, I had her send word to you that I had accepted your terms. Later, a desk and chair, some candles, a sheaf of papers and a stylus and ink were brought to my cell and I set to work. I tried many different ways to tell my tale to you, seeking to find some manner in which I could cast myself in a more flattering light. There is much that I have written since that I would rather not have, for it shows me to be the headstrong and careless fool I know myself to be.

No doubt you saw much of my handiwork: the discarded papers, the marked-out words and lines, the endless lies that I told. I should have burnt all these false trails. They served only to engender doubt in you when I at last came to the truth. For I did come to the truth in the end. There was no other way, though I feared so greatly to admit what in truth I am. But if I was to entrust my life to your keeping, as it seemed I had to, then I had no choice but to be utterly honest with you. If you discovered that I had betrayed you with my words, it would be my ruin.

It was not an easy task, as I think you know. We met each day for confession and prayer and you encouraged me to continue with my work, sensing, I'm sure, my reluctance. I had not given a thought to my days in the convent since I had left that place. My abandonment of my Sisters and María's death trouble me still. The dreams that I had once had of her returned to haunt my sleep. Before they had ended with the arrival of the Inquisitor Doctor Don Carlos de Cagarse y Carrión, but now it was the Stranger in tribunal robes who sat in judgment upon me.

I have had much to think about as I have written this confession of my many misdeeds. There are many choices that I now rue, much that was rash and foolish. I suppose it is always so with life; the path not taken seems limitless while the one we are on is soon overgrown and tangled. Enough, I will stop before I grow too maudlin.

The only person I had to speak with during my imprisonment, aside from you, was the girl Inés. The rest of your servants either feared or despised me, depending on the tales they had heard. The whole town had heard Juan de Silva's accusations by this point, of course, and I'm certain the Stranger and Don Rafael were not close-lipped when asked about me. In spite of my scurrilous reputation, the girl would talk to me when she delivered my food, and took away my dishes. We spoke mostly of inconsequential things: places I had been, the weather outside, bits and pieces of her own life that she was willing share. It was a kindness to me, one of the few that has been granted me in this miserable place, and I was so thankful to her for it.

Here I should make mention of the Widow, for it will seem as though she had vanished utterly from the earth, though only days before she had been insisting that I marry her daughter and fall under her rule. To me it was as though she had disappeared, for she was nowhere to be seen or heard—not that I would have expected her to come to my aid in these dire straits. She could not have failed to hear of my predicament—the whole town was alive with talk of it—and yet she did not step forward, either to give the lie to the accusations or to add more of her own. Why that should be I could not say, though I had my suspicions, which were later proven right.

Our own conversations after evening prayers were of much weightier matters. You saw how I was tortured by what I was writing, and no matter your protestations that you believed in my innocence, you suspected that I had much to answer for (and how right you were). How you would talk of this as an opportunity, not only to save myself from the clutches of the Stranger, but to unburden my mind and save my soul from damnation. Did you just want my confession in your hands, a dagger to be concealed against the Stranger's predations? Or were you well and truly concerned with my eternal well-being?

I am familiar enough with your ways and habits now that I think I can hazard a guess. The mean politics of the day, which you were reduced to in your dealings with both myself and the Stranger, were distasteful to you. They sullied your alliance with Our Lord, as our flesh shall always betray us. But you could justify to yourself— if not to Christ the Redeemer, for nothing can be hidden from His eyes—what you were doing, provided you could believe that I was to be saved and set upon a righteous path. A path of the Lord.

I well remember listening to you muse on the possibility of me joining a monastery after this madness was through, guided there by your compelling hand. How angered and betrayed you must have felt when you read the first pages that I gave you detailing my years in La Encarnación. I can see you turning page after page and then sitting alone, the candles burning down, the night beginning its slow turn to day, as you saw all that you had imagined turned to nothing because of the poor scratchings of this miserable wretch.

You would have told yourself that what I had written could not possibly be true. How many times had we sat together to talk of Aquinas and Torquemada, of life and eternity and the soul, and you had never suspected? How many times had you taken my hand in yours in blessing, never once noticing that it was woman's hand? You would have cursed yourself for being a fool for ever having trusted a scoundrel like me, for it seemed that all the Stranger's accusations against me were true. It was the only explanation you were able to accept before God opened your heart to forgiveness and the truth.

Worst of all would have been the thought of what I might say to the Inquisitor or the Stranger about our agreement. If I was willing to lie so brazenly to you, when my very life and freedom depended upon your trust in me, then there was no telling what I was capable of saying or doing. In that moment, as the dawn light flooded your chambers, after a tormented and sleepless night, you resolved that you would have me confess my sins, confess the truth, and help wipe the stain you saw spreading from my cell, threatening to corrupt all your earthly works. Your anger was righteous and in Our Lord's name, but at its base there was only fear that made you lash out at me. Fear that I would betray you to the Stranger. Fear that I might drag you into the Inquisition's vigilant search for any whiff of heresy or superstition to be found among us.

I am trying to explain to myself how you could have done what you did to me, knowing as you did who I am. I will not write of those dark days where it seemed I should never see the blessed sun again, where you caged and whipped me, scoured me with pincers and thumbtacks and finally, when all else had failed, rendered me mute with the pear of anguish. The dawn is coming again soon, a new dawn, and with it a new day.

What horror I endured at your hands. It seems I must relive it again, for I am compelled to write further, though each word causes me to shudder. I have no idea how long this madness lasted; the hours were unceasing in my mind. In that basement cell with no windows I could not tell the passage of the days, beyond what my body told of when I desired to sleep and wake, and even that became confused under your ministrations. Do those days trouble your sleep as they do mine? I am sure all uncertainty has been banished from your mind again and that you have convinced yourself that this was all God's will.

I did not submit to you, fool that I am. A smarter man would have. I resisted you at every turn, succeeding only in prolonging my misery. Again and again you demanded that I confess, that I tell you the truth of my origins and my nature, that I abjure my superstition and put aside my magicks. I did not, because I could not. There was no more truth to tell. It was as I had written it, as this entire account has been truthful. A lie would set me free, but I refused to go down that path, for that way was filled with darkness and traps. I would keep my faith in Our Lord to save me.

For a time I refused to speak to you or to write anymore. You still had your heart set upon using my written confession as a cudgel against the Stranger, so I was determined to deny you that so long as you persisted in your torture. This only angered you further, for each day that I delayed was a day that brought the Inquisitor closer to your door. You could hear the thunder of his horse's hooves upon the trail and it pushed you into a kind of frenzy.

I had only you to speak with for all that time. You banished all others from my world, setting a guard upon my door and bringing the bit of food and water allotted me yourself each day. I think in this way you hoped to break down my resistance. Some days you would be yourself, as I had known you, kind and gentle, a man of the cloth hoping to provide guidance through our corrupting realm. Others you would be fury itself as you attacked my flesh at its weakest points. Then there were the times you would not come at all, hours upon hours, as thirst and hunger overwhelmed me, and I cried and begged for the sight of you again.

At last you grew despondent of breaking me, as it became clear that you could destroy my body but you could not reach my soul. I held that close to me. I remember well the day, for you had left me alone for some time. Two days, I thought, though it may have been longer. All the laws of time had been suspended for me. There was only an everlasting now in which I existed. Into this hell you entered, bringing a cup of cold broth and a dried-out heel of bread, both of which I fed upon like a stray dog. You watched me at my feast, your face bathed in the shadows as you stood outside the light cast by your candles, and I could see the defeat and resignation written plain upon your face.

When I had finished you said, in a tired and dull voice: Will you end this charade at last? Will you confess your sins to me?

I have written my confession, I told you, and I will write no more until you acknowledge its truth. That is easily done. Have your women inspect me. The proof will be there for them to see.

Very well, you said with a heavy sigh, as though this were a burden you had hoped to avoid. I had hoped to gain your cooperation, but since you persist in your defiance you leave me no choice. I shall have to punish you as a liar and blasphemer.

With that you withdrew that terrible contraption, the pear of anguish, from your robes and summoned your guards to subdue me. I knew at an instant what you were about. This was not punishment, it was to silence me, so that I could not speak against you. I struggled against your men, but I was weak from the trials I had endured and you were able easily to place the pear firmly within my mouth. Without uttering another word you began to turn the screw at the instrument's end, which slowly spread apart the leaves of the pear, a bitter fruit coming to bloom in my mouth.

Each turn pressed my mouth open wider and wider. I tried to speak, to curse you, to beg you, but the instrument gagged me. You did not stop, even as my jaw began to tear apart and my soundless screams filled my head. You heard nothing but my rasping and turned the device further and further, until my jaw could go no wider, and then you turned it further still.

I remember nothing of what followed. When I awoke I was in darkness and alone, my agony unending. I wanted so desperately to scream and cry at my torment, but the slightest tremor of movement sent spasms of pain reverberating through my mind. For a long while I simply lay near oblivion, letting the waves of pain wash across me, my thoughts empty. After a time I forced myself to sit up, nearly vomiting from the discomfort as I did.

My thoughts were so bleak at that moment that I began to weep uncontrollably, for it seemed my days were at an end. I despaired of ever being free of your bonds now that you had silenced me. The Inquisitor would soon be here and I would be defenseless. Or not entirely. Upon the floor I spied the paper and ink you had left me throughout your torments in the hopes that I would submit to your demands. And so in the darkness, nearly blinded by my suffering, I started again upon my chronicle, hoping to bring some light into this bleak place.

I wrote in a fever through the night and the next day, only barely aware of the passage of time and the dull throb of my shattered jaw, until at last my exhaustion became too much and I threw myself down upon my poor bed to sleep. Your conscience must have worked upon you, for when I awoke your guards were emptying the room of your infernal devices. After they had gone there was a knock at the door and Inés entered, bringing with her a bowl of broth and some wine.

My heart leapt to see her after so many days when I had been left to suffer alone. I was so overwhelmed by emotion and the struggles of those last weeks that I am ashamed to say I wept as she took my hands in hers. She proved her kindness that day, for in spite of all that she had heard of my crimes, she took me into her arms and comforted me. When I had recovered myself she fed me the broth, taking great care that I did not suffer too much in the act, though the pain even of swallowing was nearly unbearable.

After I had eaten we talked for a time—or, more accurately, she whispered to me of the world beyond these walls, and I wrote my questions and responses upon the paper you had provided me. She had much to tell me, for it seemed the Stranger had the entire city in an uproar, having seized control of the Audiencia and threatened the Alcalde and others with charges of corruption. You feared that you would next, I suspect, which added to the frenzy with which you had tried to break me before the Inquisitor arrived. But I thwarted you, though it cost me greatly, for the last piece of news Inés had for me was that the Inquisitor had arrived that very morning.

The news spurred me to action and I continued to write, hoping to have all of my tale written before he was brought to seek my confession. But he was not the next to visit me. That night, even as I wrote of the long days of my sanctuary in San Sebastién, the Stranger called upon me. I was so focused upon my scratchings that I did not hear the door unlock; it was only the movement of the shadows that announced his presence. That and his foul stench, which saved me from having to turn to look upon him.

Making a last confession, he said as he shut the door firmly behind him. Have no fear, you shall not perish. I shall see to it.

As he said it he seized me by the chin and turned me around so that I was forced to look upon his terrible eyes. The pain was so great that my senses left me, but he slapped me awake, sending me into a fit of pitiful moans and seizures. At last he released my broken face and stood up, looking down on me as though I were a wayward mongrel at last returned to its master.

Though it cost me dearly, and my voice was hardly audible, I asked him: Why not kill me now?

He laughed and said: I am not so kind capon. That is what you want, after all, to escape this punishment no matter what means you must use. I will not let you. We have not finished what we started that night in the crypt. I will see you bound to me in body and I will devour your soul.

I trembled at his words, for I could well recall the automata enslaved to Don Francisco in his infernal ceremony.

As if understanding my very thoughts, the Stranger said: You are familiar with the work of my friend from Paita. I do not require you to be quite so docile. I am willing to allow you to submit to me freely. I think you will capon. Our kind does not fare well with the Inquisition.

I have nothing to fear from the Inquisition, I said to him, my voice sounding even more enfeebled than it already was.

The Stranger laughed again. We shall see, he said.

I summoned what courage and strength was left in me and asked him a question that had long been on my mind during my imprisonment: Did you come here in search of me?

No, he said, it was a happy confluence of events. I am not a Visitor of the Crown, as you will no doubt have already guessed. These fools will not realize it until it is far too late.

You are the fool, I said to him. They already plot against you.

Oh, I know of their plans, he said to me. I have compatriots who intercept any letter that leaves this place, and others who will write replies for me from the Crown. It is all neatly done. Soon you will join them in service to me, as will all grandees of this town. I nearly had Cuzco in my possession before you killed Don Lope and the others. But my designs outstripped my ability there, sadly. Here, a city not without wealth, but on the empire's edge. Here I can settle without fear.

I will never submit to you, I said to him, as tears burned my eyes and my hands trembled.

Look how your hands shake, he said. What you have endured is just a beginning. Once the Inquisitor has had his way there will be no more superstition within you.

Another man to do your bidding, I said to him bitterly.

On the contrary, the Stranger said, Doctor Don Carlos de Cagarse y Carrión is a man of pure and singular intent. Incorruptible. And as I say, our kind does not fare well in their eyes. That is why I asked for him. You think you have known suffering, but you do not know what suffering is. Before he is through you will beg me to save you, and perhaps I will.

He intended these, his final words to me, to land like a blow, and I certainly gave him reason to think it had been so, as I would not meet his eyes and cowered before him. But as soon as he left me and the door was closed and locked behind him, I smiled, for a slender ray of hope had penetrated within my dark cell. He feared me—not nearly as much as I feared him, and with good reason, but enough that he could not risk leaving things to chance and had called upon those who he was certain could bring me to heel. There had been hard experience voiced in his words on the Inquisition, and he was right to fear them for he had committed many crimes against Our Lord. But in doing so he had brought a man into the game who was not his to play. A man I knew well, for I had gone before him to confess long ago. If anyone could believe my claims as to who I was, it would be him.

There is little time left for this indulgence now, so I will not tarry. It provided a welcome distraction in those bleak hours when I could see no way out of this prison but my own abnegation. Now that my salvation lies at hand, I must turn my mind to other matters. Little remains to be told.

For two days after the Stranger's visit I awaited the arrival of Doctor Don Carlos de Cagarse y Carrión to confess me. My only visitor was the lovely and kind Inés, who continued to nurse me to health. She told me that you had worked to delay the doctor's audience with me until you could be certain the confession would go as you wished. Events, it seemed, had overtaken your plans, with stories of my presence in your home beginning to spread like wildfire through Tucumán.

How many of the souls in your house did you let pass within the door of my cell before you sealed me there to conduct your nefarious torture? How many more did I encounter on those evenings when I was brought to confess to you? Nearly all, and you thought nothing of it, for you noticed none of them and what they do. They exist only in service to you, as far as you are concerned. But they see and hear all, and if at first their hearts were hard toward me, I was able to soften many of them, to the point that, when you began your most unjust actions upon my flesh, they rebelled.

At the same time, as they began to spread stories of my unjust imprisonment, word of the true nature of the Stranger became common gossip. Any Visitor, even a false one such as he, will not be popular with those of standing within a city, and all those who resented his seizure of the Audiencia and his other investigations seized upon his involvement in the accusations against me as evidence that he was acting falsely. In his arrogance the Stranger did himself no favors, consorting about town with Juan de Silva at his side at all times, as though the scoundrel was his familiar. There were dark whispers as to the nature of their relationship, and Don Luis let it be known that he considered me innocent and Don Juan's accusations against me false.

By the time the Inquisitor arrived, the whole city was aflame with the idea that a woman, falsely accused by the strange Visitor Don Miguel and his companion Juan de Silva, was being held and tortured by you to extract a false confession before the Inquisitor could do his work. This, I am sure, terrified you to no end. You had realized, too late, that it was well known about town that you were in league with the devils and that all you had said and done within these walls was common knowledge. Inevitably the Inquisitor would hear such talk, and if what I had confessed to you was in fact true, if I was a woman, then you had to know you were doomed.

All this I learned from Inés, and it gladdened my heart, for I knew you would have to assure yourself that I was not what I claimed to be before you could let me before Doctor Don Carlos de Cagarse y Carrión. How well I knew you! On the second day after the Stranger's visit, two of your women, as well as Inés, called upon me and had me disrobe before them. They inspected me thoroughly, taking great care to look over all my womanly parts, and then left me to dress again.

I set myself to writing my tale again, my heart alight, for I could not see how you could deny what they had seen. Two others, whom I did not recognize, came that evening and had me disrobe again. I asked one of them who they were and she said she was a midwife.

And what do think of what you have seen, I asked her.

You are a women as God created you, she said, and I agreed that I was.

The next morning you called upon me, not long after Inés had brought me my meal of broth. Your face was white as a ghost as you looked upon me and my broken face, so badly disfigured. I was growing quite sallow by then as well, for you had fed me little during your torture sessions, and now I could hardly manage to sup upon a bowl of soup. You seemed timid and unsure of what to say, and I let you suffer.

At last you summoned what courage you had and said: I am sorry. It seems I was wrong to doubt you.

I nodded my thanks and waited, staring up at you. You could not meet my eyes, and I would have smiled if the pain had not been so great.

Doctor Don Carlos de Cagarse y Carrión will arrive tomorrow to hear your confession, you said, swallowing loudly. You have heard he has arrived, I am sure.

In answer I reached into my shirt and pulled out a piece of paper, on which I had written some words. I watched as you read them carefully, your eyes scanning to the bottom and then starting at the top again.

I agree, you said, provided you take off these false trappings and dress as a woman properly should.

I nodded and handed you a pen and you wrote your signature upon the page, and then I added mine. You left immediately after that, as though you could not bear a moment further in my presence. Inés came later that evening to move me into the room I now occupy. It is a lovely place, suitable for any guest, with a soft bed and, most importantly for me, a window. I am looking out it now upon the darkness, the moon nearly full above. It calls to me, but my work here is not yet done.

Although I have the document, which we both signed, I will record what I wrote here as part of my confession so that there can be no question as to what we put our names to:

Don Juan Bautista de Arteaga, Bishop of Tucumán, I have

much reason both to hate and mistrust you, but now is not the time to allow such grievances to stand between us. We share a common enemy, the man you call Don Miguel, Visitor of the Crown to this fine city. He is the reason for my imprisonment and why you refused to believe me when I confessed truthfully before you and in the eyes of Our Lord.

Your women have inspected me and there can be no doubt as to the veracity of my words. I have written the rest of my confession and it contains much as to the true nature of the man you call Don Miguel. He is a devil made flesh. I know he has accused me of being able to transmute myself, among other such foul magicks, but I can tell you for a fact that it is he who is the possessor of such terrible faculties. You suspect as much yourself, I am sure, as do many others in this town, if the stories that have reached my ears are any evidence.

There is much more of which you are unaware. The man has confessed to me that he is not a Visitor of the Crown and that he travels under false letters. Not only that, he plots with one of the landowners to the west of here to seize great tracts of land from both you and your friend Don Rafael. This landowner, of whom I am intimately familiar, knows that you obtained it illegally from its rightful owners and Don Miguel will use his powers as Visitor to see that it is taken from you and falls into their hands, or those of their allies. With that wealth and with all the officials who might oppose him either cowed or removed, he will rule this town. If he is allowed to do this you will never remove him, I can assure you, for his powers are great.

What I offer to you is my true and complete confession to the Inquisitor. I shall tell him these things and others that I know the man you call Don Miguel to be guilty of. I shall blame your part in this sordid affair upon his infernal influence over you and others in this town. In exchange for this I ask only that I be allowed to speak to the Inquisitor immediately, so that I may make my confession fully and that I be given a room befitting that of a guest rather than a prisoner.

Yours in faith, Luisa.

I have left this final part of my confession where I am certain someone will find it. I do not know whether it will be you or Don Carlos who will be reading this, but whoever it is all will be explained here. By now I have long departed your residence and Tucumán.

The rest, the true document and confession, is with Don Carlos. I gave it to him this morning when he invited me to confess. I had taken on a woman's dress by then, as you had demanded, and of course he remembered me. He had heard of my strange disappearance from La Encarnación and was quite taken aback to discover that I had somehow ended up here all these years later. His suspicions were aroused as well, for he has always been a skeptical man. I feel quite certain that he had suspected me of some misdeed in the convent, but could simply not prove that I had done wrong.

I testified to him that I remained a virgin through all my adventures and gave him my true testament, which he read. When he had finished he studied me with his careful eyes, his face expressionless, and said: Do you swear before God that all that is written here is true?

I do, I said aloud, though it pained me.

There are many troubling matters in here, he said, foremost among them this man, the Stranger, as you refer to him. You say this man is the same Don Miguel who is Visitor of the Crown here in this city, and that he is a fraud.

I said that was indeed so.

And the Bishop, he said, he refused to accept your confession before God?

He did, I said.

Don Carlos leaned forward so that his face was nearly pressed into mine, his eyes peering directly into my own as though he might see within my soul. He said to me: There are many troubling hints here about your own nature. Don Miguel seems to view you as a kindred spirit. As I recall, there were many in La Encarnación who felt you unnatural and a practitioner of the arts of superstition.

Though it was very difficult and I had to speak slowly, with tears forming in my eyes, I said to him: Those accusations by my Sisters were nothing but mean rumors. You yourself proved them false. They, and the death of my dear friend, are why I had to leave the convent. I could stomach it no longer. Since then I have done many things, had many adventures and have much to answer for before God. I am willing to do that penance, but I have done nothing that is heretical or superstitious. I stand within the faith as always.

This satisfied him, at least for the moment, and he sent me away, saying that I was to stay here in your house until his investigation was complete. That afternoon Inés brought word to me that the Stranger had been arrested and was being held in the same jail where Don Luis had laid me to the rack. The walls there are sturdy, and I am certain Don Carlos has ensured he has no window through which to slip out. He will be there for a long while, I imagine, and it will not go well. Juan de Silva will turn upon him, as will some of his other conspirators.

Don Carlos has in all likelihood spoken to you of what I have written, and you will be most surprised to find out that there is much in this document on what you had done to me. Did you not think I knew when you slipped into my cell those nights after the Stranger had told you I had begun my writing again and took away the pages to read them, carefully replacing them before morning? After all, the night is my companion more than it is yours, as my words have made plain. Did you not realize that Inés told me that you had forced her to confess all that we had spoken of? She is made of sterner stuff than you realize, and she told you but a part, just as I did in those pages that you read.

There were two copies written—one the truth, one for your benefit. I hoped to convince you to allow me to see the Inquisitor, for I feared ever being allowed to speak so long as you were concerned that I might confess all that had happened in that cell. Would I have perished under mysterious circumstances the night before my audience with Don Carlos? I think it likely, though you will deny it to your final breath. So two documents seemed prudent—one I hid well, one I left for you to find and set your mind at ease. You will have much to answer for in the days to come.

Why have I left, then, now that I hold a sword above your head and the Stranger, Juan de Silva and the Widow Márquez are all trapped in cells? For one, I knew you were going to betray me, to accuse me of idolatry and other things, once I had made my confession and the Stranger was safely imprisoned. You could not risk having me about, knowing what I knew of your false dealings with Don Rafael and of what you had done to me. Even now that I am far from your sight I am certain you will be working strenuously to discredit all I have written of you, while claiming the truth of all I have said of the Stranger.

The second reason can be found in the final name, which I have just revealed to you. Perhaps you have guessed it already, for I did little to disguise her identity in my narrative. At any rate, you will recognize it and know her well, for her daughter is in your employ. You cannot imagine my delight when I discovered that Inés was among your servants. At last I had met the Widow's daughter and could understand why she had been so desperate to seal our betrothal. For, as you know, the Widow Márquez is Inés' stepmother and she had worked hard to deny her daughter her rightful inheritance, exiling her to your home where you kept her as your servant.

How incestuous your relations are and how false. You accuse me of dishonor, and yet it is you who has put upon the mask of honor to disguise your misdeeds. Inés has told me what you promised her, that you would help her regain her inheritance so wrongly taken from her. Yet it was you who conspired with the Widow to take it from her in the first place. And it was you, along with the Widow and Don Rafael, who conspired to take the land of many others. With Inés in your possession you saw an opportunity to lay claim to the Widow's lands as well. She was wise enough not to trust you, which was why she sought to take advantage of my appearance. If she could have sealed my marriage to Inés, and kept her influence over me, then you would have had nothing to hold over her.

The arrival of the Stranger changed everything, and she threw in her lot with him. He had the authority of the Crown, however falsely gained, and she the secrets that he could use against authorities such as yourself. I was the only problem. The Stranger did not think he could kill me, and he feared to let the matter play out in the courts of the Audiencia; why, I do not know. Instead he summoned the Inquisition, sealing his own doom. Such men who gain by fear are ruled by it in all their thoughts.

How did I come to know all this while sealed within the cell, under guard and lock and key? It was a simple matter. You looked at me and saw one thing when in fact I was another. It was the same with your servant Inés. You thought her an ignorant and pitiful child, brought to heel and of no consequence in this greater game you were playing. She passed through the world unseen, as I have often have, for who pays any mind to a woman of no importance? You forever see what you want, not the truth of the thing.

But I saw her for what she was: a kindhearted woman of singular beauty that had been driven from her face by all of you who had treated her as little more than a piece upon a board, to be moved as you saw fit. For a time she believed it of herself, that she was but a pawn to be sacrificed, until I showed her the truth of the matter. She was a queen who could determine her own fate and she has chosen to do so at my side. For that I am happier than I could ever have imagined.

But I have no more time for this. Inés is at my door and we must leave now before we are discovered. I look forward to the days to come as we make our way freely through this strange and glorious world.

Written by my hand in the year of Our Lord 1605

EXCERPT:

THE TRIALS OF THE MINOTAUR

In the fifth year of the rule of Auten the One Eyed a minotaur is born to one of Colosi's most important families.

Taken from his mother as a newborn, exiled and cast from his family, the minotaur vows to return to the imperial city and take his rightful place as a patrician in the empire. But the patriarch of the family, his grandfather, will stop at nothing to see this blemish to his honor destroyed.

And so begins an epic journey, through lands beyond imagining, marked by despair and exile, triumph and betrayal. At its heart lies a quest to be free.

IT WAS IN THE FIFTH year of the rule of Auten the One-Eyed, the emperor of Rheadd during the second interregnum, that a minotaur was born to the daughter of an important patrician family, the Dethcalla. They have long had the ear of the emperor so it will surprise no one that nearly all mention of the Minotaur has been excised from the official chronicles of the day. However, a careful search of some of the more scandalous histories of the period does produce some mentions of the creature. That the creature existed cannot be doubted for, though unnamed, it is on the patrician rolls.

No one knew how Surys Dethcallen Barthil, the daughter of Barthil Dethcallan Vulgih, had come to be with child, for she was unmarried and no more than fourteen. The Dethcalla had naturally followed the correct practice at every turn in her upbringing, and her education was impeccable. To the best knowledge of the nurse and eunuch charged with her keep, she had never been on the streets of Colosi, the imperial capital, unescorted or uncovered.

Once her father, a dour and forbidding soul, discovered her state, he strove to keep the facts of her condition as obscure as possible in an effort to avoid a scandal. The girl was not seen in public company, which was not unusual, for the unmarried daughters of important patricians rarely were anyway. He had her taken to his summer estate under the cover of darkness and amid much secrecy for her to carry the pregnancy to term over the fall and winter. He left only a few of his most trusted servants to see to her care, with strict instructions and the threat of execution that they should speak to no one.

If all had gone to plan the child would have disappeared to some orphanage in one of the distant imperial provinces, never to gain knowledge of its patrician birthright, with the rest of Colosi none the wiser. The child, however, came early, while Barthil Vulgih was still attending at court, his business and duty public. The last thing he wanted to do was to draw attention by fleeing the city, so he waited until the matters were resolved and then left to dispose of the child.

By the time he arrived, three days after he had received the message, there were six census officials awaiting him at the gate to add the newborn to the patrician rolls. Though furious beyond measure, Barthil could hardly deny them entrance, for the law required that all those of noble blood be recorded on the rolls. To deny the child's existence could only result in prosecution by his enemies, one of whom had surely had a hand in engineering this predicament.

He noticed the strained and fearful glances of the servants who had been charged with his daughter's care as he passed by them to her chambers, but gave it no thought. The presence of the census notaries meant that one of them had betrayed him, so all would be fearful for their lives. The notaries allowed him a moment with his daughter and grandchild before they entered to make their record. He left them outside the door with the child's wet nurse, who would not meet his eyes.

At first he did not believe what he saw nestled in his daughter's arms. He could see nothing of the body, for it was wrapped in swaddling, but its head defied all belief. The nose was broad and pink—a snout, in a word—while the ears extended from both sides of its head and moved of their own accord at his approach. The eyes were spread apart on either side of its face and it was covered in hair, all of it, thick and deep and brown.

Barthil Vulgih found himself trembling as he walked up beside the bed, his daughter looking sleepily up at him from where she lay. He thought perhaps this was a dream, a nightmare from which he might soon wake. The girl drew the creature closer to her breast as though to protect it, but he cursed her and tore it from her arms. He drew it up to his eyes, contemplating the now squalling beast, considering as he did so that he should put an end to the creature's life then and there, no matter the prosecution he would be forced to endure. He knew though that there was no use, there could be no erasing this stain to the family's honor.

"You are the ruin of this family," he said, though whether it was directed to the beast or his daughter was unclear. He noticed that the creature had two nubs, almost obscured by its hair atop its head, and ran a finger distractedly over one, realizing they were the beginnings of the thing's horns. Something between a sob and a roar emerged from his throat.

When he had regained his composure he carried the newborn to the door, which he threw open, startling the waiting census officials. They stared at the crying thing in Barthil Vulgih's hands with horror and then did their utmost to avoid looking at either of the beast or the patrician, occupying themselves with their official scrolls and their ink and pens. The servants refused to glance over as well, though the creature's wails grew louder and louder. The ostentatious obliviousness displayed by all those present only served to increase the rage consuming Barthil Vulgih.

One of the notaries cleared his throat, though he still would not raise his eyes from the rolls. "You confirm that the date of birth was the seventh day of Gethuj?"

"I do," Barthil Vulgih said in a voice that made all in his presence shudder.

"And the name chosen for the child?"

"It will have none."

This caused both census officials to stare at the patriarch, their mouths agape.

"It must have a name," one of them said at last. "It is on the rolls."

"It will have none," Barthil Vulgih repeated, and then turned on his heel and strode back into his daughter's chambers, flinging the door shut behind him. He paced back and forth across the room, the beast still crying in his arms, but he did not seem to notice it or his daughter, who watched him without uttering a word.

This continued for some time until one of the guards knocked at the door. When there was no answer he summoned the courage to enter, but Barthil Vulgih did not even glance at him, so lost was he in his anguished thoughts. The guard cleared his throat and then, when that too failed to draw his master's attention, he called out his name. This did rouse the patrician, who stopped on his heels and stared at the guard in fury and bewilderment.

"The census officials have left, sir," the guard said, and

swallowed.

Barthil Vulgih nodded and then walked over to his daughter, returning the creature to her. "Good," he said. "I want you and your men to put to death every servant and eunuch here. One of them has betrayed me."

The guard nodded and had turned to go when the girl spoke. "I sent for them," she said.

Barthil Vulgih looked at her without emotion, as though contemplating the tithes on one of his distant and unimportant estates.

"I knew you would take him from me. Now you cannot close your door to him. He is on the rolls, he is of this family."

Barthil Vulgih did not say anything and left the room, the guard falling in step behind him. His reply came later that day as all thirteen servants and two eunuchs were led, one by one, to his daughter's room, where they were beheaded. She did not look away from the executions, facing them with the same emotionless stare her father had fixed on her, even as the stain on the floor continued to grow. Neither would speak another word to the other the rest of their days.

The Trials of the Minotaur is now available.

ABOUT THE AUTHOR

Clint Westgard is the author of The Shadow Men Trilogy and the science fiction epic The Sojourner Cycle, the first volume of which, The Forgotten, was published in 2015. In addition, he has published a work of historical fantasy set in colonial Peru, The Maleficio Chronicles, and a retelling of the Minotaur legend, The Trials of the Minotaur. Clint Westgard lives in Calgary, Alberta.

ALSO BY CLINT WESTGARD

Realm of Shadows
Volume One of The Shadow Men

Craitol and Renuih, two empires a world apart, divided by the desert that lies between them. A desert ruled by the Shadow Men.

An uneasy peace holds sway in both realms, hiding longstanding feuds and bitter rivalries. Until a Shadow Men raid on Renuih shatters the calm and sets in motion events no one can control.

Masiph id Ezern, unfavored son of the Imperial Vazeir, finds himself a hero following the raid. His father remains unmoved by his exploits and, in his bitterness, Masiph will find himself a reluctant participant in a plot against the empire.

As he finds himself drawn deeper and deeper into the conspiracy, he soon realizes there will be no escaping the realm of shadows, where intrigue and betrayal abound. And though the Shadow Men have gone quiet, they will not stay silent forever...

ALSO BY CLINT WESTGARD

Council of Shadows
Volume Two of The Shadow Men

Discontent continues to fester within the realms of Craitol and Renuih, fed by intrigues carried out in the shadows. As rivals and apostates struggle for supremacy, a long incubated plan begins to unfold.

Vyissan, a mysterious alkemycal practitioner arrives in Renuih, the latest strike in a long war over who shall control the secrets of alkemya and Craitol itself. He carries with him a secret that, once revealed, will reverberate across all realms. Before he can reveal it though, the conspirators against the emperor will strike their own blow.

But now, a new and more powerful menace looms on the horizon. The Shadow Men have gained the secrets of the Council Adept's alkemya and no one can be certain what they will do with it...

ALSO BY CLINT WESTGARD

Dance of Shadows
Volume Three of The Shadow Men

War with the Shadow Men looms in both realms as the consequences of the Gvers' Council in Craitol begin to make themselves known. A war that could end in glorious triumph or bitter disaster.

Doubt shadows everyone's steps, for they know there are no certainties in the desert. Especially now the Shadow Men have made the art of alkemya their own.

No one has more questions than Vyissan, for he is working in service to a cause he is no longer sure he believes in. And now he must undertake a journey with those who both loathe and fear him. Before the first sword is drawn, his life will be under threat.

But his will not be the only one, for somewhere in the desert the Shadow Men lie in wait…

ALSO BY CLINT WESTGARD

The Forgotten
Volume One of The Sojourners Cycle

Who is David Aeida? And what does he know that has so many
people pursuing him?

David doesn't know. He can't remember anything about who he is.
But he finds himself ensnared in a vicious conflict between a
religious cult and a guild that patrols the crossings between
multiple universes. They will both stop at nothing to gain whatever
knowledge he possesses. Most dangerous of all, is the implacable
hunter, known only as the Seeker, who has his own reasons for
wanting to find David.

His only hope is to recover his memories before they do. His only
ally is a woman named Meredith, and she definitely knows more
than she is telling…

Spanning both universes and the human mind, The Forgotten is an
unforgettable science fiction thriller that questions the very nature
of identity. It is the first volume of the Sojourners Cycle, an epic
that will encompass the fates of universes and humanity itself.

ALSO BY CLINT WESTGARD

The Apostate
Volume Two of The Sojourners Cycle

Laila has only one goal in mind. To have her revenge upon the Grand Regent for all he has done to her. First, though, she needs to find her way across the universes.

That is easier said than done. The Grand Regent's agents are still pursuing her. As is the Society of Travellers. And the Seeker lurks somewhere, waiting for his moment to strike.

Laila has a plan, though, and a few tricks of her own. But she will discover that not everything is at seems. For the war she has given her life to hides a far greater conflict.

Spanning multiple universes and the complexities of the human mind, The Apostate, continues the incredible journey begun in The Forgotten. The second volume of The Sojourners Cycle is an unforgettable science fiction epic that encompasses the fates of universes and humanity itself.

ALSO BY CLINT WESTGARD

The Trials of the Minotaur

In the fifth year of the rule of Auten the One Eyed a minotaur is born to one of Colosi's most important families.

Taken from his mother as a newborn, exiled and cast from his family, the minotaur vows to return to the imperial city and take his rightful place as a patrician in the empire. But the patriarch of the family, his grandfather, will stop at nothing to see this blemish to his honor destroyed.

And so begins an epic journey, through lands beyond imagining, marked by despair and exile, triumph and betrayal. At its heart lies a quest to be free.

ALSO BY CLINT WESTGARD

The Devious Kind

A Mystery

The body of a local woman is found in a coulee on a ranch north of Loverna, her head blown off with a shotgun. New to town and the job, Constable Martin Thomas arrives on the scene as a spring snowstorm begins to wipe out all evidence before his investigation has even begun.

There is no shortage of suspects to consider. A spurned husband. A jealous lover. A betrayed business partner. And family members battling over an inheritance. All have motive and opportunity. And no one seems to be telling him everything.

As he tries to sift the truth from the lies, the snowstorm continues to build, leaving Loverna cut off from the outside world. And Thomas alone to face a killer who will do anything not to get caught.